Copyright © 2021 Cara Maxwell

All rights reserved. No part of this book may be reproduced, or stored in a retrieval system, or transmitted in any form or by any means, electronic, mechanical, photocopying, recording, or otherwise, without express written permission of the publisher.

For permissions contact:
caramaxwellromance@gmail.com

This is a work of fiction. Names, characters, places, and incidents either are the product of the author's imagination or are used fictitiously. Any resemblance to actual persons, living or dead, events, or locales is entirely coincidental.

Cover by: Forever After Romance Designs
Edited by: A. Fischer

To my dear friend Ashley,
for always saying it like it is.

Cara Maxwell

Racing Rogues
Book 1

Chapter 1

He had to win.
Eric Weathers had spent a small fortune to get them here – horse and rider on the racecourse, star trainer at the rail. It had to pay off.
It had to.
"He looks good, my lord."
The horse and rider were still on the flat portion of the course. They started out at a more leisurely pace, fast but sustainable. By most standards it was a winning pace.
"Good is not going to be good enough."
The ground was ideal today. It hadn't rained for several days and the turf was firm. Perfect racing conditions. But there was never any guarantee of ideal weather. In April, in England, the exact opposite was true.
"He's picking up the pace, just as I instructed him."

The pair had reached the Dip – the fall and rise of ground that comprised the last two furlongs of the Rowley Mile. Even without a pocket watch in his hand Eric knew they were going to break their personal record. He felt his heart starting to beat faster. Maybe this was going to work after all.

As they approached the post, the sound of hooves and horse got louder. They roared past the two men watching at the rail.

"Minute forty-nine."

Eric let out a long exhale. It was fast. Perhaps fast enough.

"He'll run even better when there's another horse beside him," Taylor said, still leaning forward on the rail. His eyes were following the horse and rider, who had slowed to a trot and were circling back around. "He's a competitive bugger."

"Sounds a bit like his trainer," Eric said drolly. His arms were crossed, as they had been for the entire ride. But some of the tension had gone out of him. It was a good time. Better than good. Just like he had said – better than good was what it would take.

Taylor just grunted. He straightened up as the big chestnut horse and rider came up in front of them.

"He was fast, I felt it," Tommy said confidently from aboard the colt. When Taylor told him just how fast he let out a loud '*whoop*' of excitement. "And he had more to give. I could feel it."

"Hand him over to the groom. We can discuss it while they walk him out." Taylor motioned forward the roughly clad lad who was waiting a few paces away. Other trainers and riders were starting to look at them. There was a certain level of comradery in

One Race to Ruin 3

training and racing, but ultimately it was a competition. No need to give anyone an edge.

"The start was a little slow. We don't want to risk him getting boxed in," Taylor said as the three men fell into step walking away from the track.

"I could have asked him for more sooner, sir. But I thought you wanted me to hold him back," Tommy said.

"Yes, I wanted to see how much ground he could pick up on the rise. But when we take him out next we'll have to push him sooner. To see if he can hold on."

The exercise rider nodded in agreement. "I will talk with Chester before I leave today, sir. I will let him know how the ride was."

Eric had been listening along. He trusted Jackson Taylor. He was a very well-respected trainer. Eric had paid an ungodly sum to steal him away from the Marquess of Hexham. It had almost physically hurt to part with such an amount, with the earldom in the state that it was. But it was an investment, Eric told himself. And thus far, more than two months in, he had agreed with everything the man said. But now his ears perked up.

"Talk with Chester? Why?"

"This is my last day, my lord," Tommy answered. "I gave my notice to Mr. Taylor a few weeks ago …"

"We will find another exercise rider, Tommy. Chester can handle him," Taylor put in.

Eric scoffed aloud. "Are we talking about the same horse?"

"He's going to have to take a jockey soon. We need to start accustoming him to other riders," Taylor said boldly. But glancing over, Eric could see the look on his face. He spoke with confidence but the crease in his brow betrayed his worry.

Sighing, Eric looked back over his shoulder to where the groom was walking Mercury out. The huge chestnut colt was shaking his head, pulling at his reins as the young man walked. He was the most promising horse in Eric's stable. And he had a reputation as a damnable tyrant. "Are you sure I cannot convince you to stay, Tommy?" Eric said wistfully, already bracing himself to expend another uncomfortable sum.

"I'm sorry, my lord. I've taken a job with a stable up in Doncaster."

Eric gritted his teeth. "I'm sure I can match what they've offered you. Or better it."

Tommy shook his head regretfully. "I'm that sorry, sir. But it's not a matter of pay this time. My wife's kin are from Yorkshire. Her mam's not well. She wants to be nearer with the young'uns."

"I see." Eric crossed his arms again, the tension returning. They would have to find a new exercise rider. Who could manage this hellion of a horse? Despite the turning in his stomach he knew that Taylor was right. If they were going to run Mercury in the 2000 Guineas he would need a proper jockey. The damn horse needed to learn to accept a new rider. And the sooner the better. "Well, I wish you and your family the best, Tommy. You've certainly done good work on that monster."

Despite being a middle-aged man, Tommy pinkened. It wasn't every day one got a compliment from an earl. "Thank you, sir." He tipped his cap respectfully.

Taylor cleared his throat, ready to steer the conversation back to the topic of strategy. "We need to get him out there with another horse. Perhaps we can pull Dynasty up next time and run them together, see how they play off each other –"

"Look out!"

"What the hell?"

"Someone grab that animal!"

They all started at the shouts around them and then the sound of hoofbeats came from behind, pounding past the three men.

"What the –" Eric turned just in time to see the flash of red-gold horse fly past them. "Hell and damnation!"

Tommy looked stunned, his eyes wide. Taylor was whistling as loud as he could, trying to call the horse to heel. Mercury's ears flicked back at the sound but his gait didn't falter. He was cantering alongside the track, while grooms, trainers, exercise riders, stable boys, and owners jumped out of his way. Even at a canter he was wicked fast.

"He's going to get injured! What the hell happened?" Eric turned back to where the groom had been leading the horse. The man was on the ground, a small coterie of others gathered around him. *Damn, damn, damn.* "What are we going to do?"

"We just have to let him run it out and hope the damn beast doesn't hurt himself." Taylor ignored the groom on the ground behind them and jogged after Mercury.

Eric felt the familiar ache in his stomach turn into something much sharper. *Was he never going to get a break?* He opened his mouth to speak "But—"

Another horse pounded past them, making all of them jump. Bystanders continued to jump out of the way as the horse, this one a dark bay, charged after the chestnut. At least this horse was mounted by a compact rider, Eric thought to himself. Though not one he recognized.

The horse and rider were moving at a full gallop. They came up alongside Mercury, who was still loping along at a canter. If the chestnut colt had been galloping himself catching him would have been impossible. Eric recognized the dark bay from his own stable. It was the very horse that Taylor had just mentioned – Dynasty. The four-year-old was much more even-tempered than the fiery Mercury. And he had just been on his way out for his morning exercise so he had energy to spare.

Eric wasn't sure if it made him feel better or worse that now two of his horses were running pell-mell across Newmarket. At least if this came to disaster he wouldn't have to pay out another owner, he thought practically. But he could not afford to lose two of his best horses, either. Or this whole endeavor would end as quickly as it had started.

"He'll try and grab the reins," Taylor said. "To get ahold of Mercury."

As they watched, that was exactly what the rider aboard Dynasty tried to do. He leaned over and tried to catch the reins which were swinging wildly from Mercury's neck. But the horse seemed to sense a game; he shook his head and pranced away. The rider brought Dynasty closer and tried again. Mercury responded by increasing the speed of his canter. He was reaching for a gallop and enjoying the competition.

One Race to Ruin

The rider brought Dynasty closer still. But this time he did not try to reach for the other horse's reins. He steered the dark bay closer and closer, as if they were running alongside each other at the rail like they would in a race. Even from a distance Eric saw the change in his stance, as the mysterious rider raised himself higher in the saddle.

It happened in a flash. The instant that the rider's body left the saddle there was a collective gasp from everyone watching. This was about to get a whole lot worse. And then suddenly, as if by magic, the rider was atop Mercury. Eric thought he might fall over. He had never seen such a thing in his life.

"I'll be damned," Taylor said beside him. The two men came to a stop, both stunned by what they had just witnessed.

Ever the gentleman, Dynasty was slowing to a trot and then a walk. He shook his dark head and turned from side to side as if looking for the rider that had gone missing from his back.

Now aboard Mercury, the mysterious rider managed to get ahold of the horse's reins. Mercury fought for a few seconds and then steadied. The horse slowed to a canter and then a trot. And then the rider was bringing him around, completely in hand.

Eric and Taylor reached Dynasty at the same time that the rider brought Mercury alongside. The two horses touched noses, snorting and pawing their hooves at the ground as if congratulating each other on a grand adventure.

"That was some fine riding, young man," Taylor did not hesitate or hold back his praise. He grabbed ahold of the chestnut's reins, holding his bridle firmly and slapping the rider's knee congratulatorily.

"Thank you, sir."

Once Taylor had the horse firmly in hand the rider jumped down.

He was small, like all exercise riders and jockeys were. They had to be to meet the weight limits for the races. Eric noted that the young man was better dressed than most exercise riders he had met. He wore tawny breeches that were mostly clean, a cream-colored shirt, leather riding gloves, and a hunter green linen vest that was buttoned up over his shirt. His tweed cap was pulled low over his head. Perhaps the younger son of a middle-class family. Not taking on the family business, but certainly benefiting from it.

"Lord Fordham, this is Dani. We've just brought him on trial today." Taylor introduced the young man. As the lad turned his face up to the tall lord, Eric realized he was not much more than a boy.

"I owe you a great deal of thanks, Dani." Eric held out his hand. The young man stared at it, then extended his own awkwardly. Eric shook it, noting that the boy-man kept his eyes downcast. "You've saved me a significant investment, young man."

"He's a fine horse, sir," Dani said. His voice was still rather high-pitched.

"He's a pain in the arse," Taylor cut in. "But you've got a way with him. I hope you don't mind, my lord, if I take on young Dani here on a more permanent basis."

Dani flushed, an eager look in his young, dark eyes.

"I would say it is well earned," Eric agreed. "How old are you, boy? And where in the world did you learn to ride like that?"

The young man looked away and cleared his throat awkwardly. "I am nineteen, sir." Eric almost laughed

One Race to Ruin

aloud. There was no way. But he stuffed the impulse down as the young man continued to speak. "My mother was from Spain, sir. She taught me to ride in the Spanish style, sir."

He was being a bit effusive with the 'sirs.' He'd probably never met a member of the nobility, Eric thought to himself. Well, that hardly mattered. Gentility meant nothing aboard a horse, especially one with a temperament like Mercury. There was something else about the young man that made Eric want to look closer but he did not get the chance to explore that thought.

"You've found a rider to take my place!" Tommy said enthusiastically, joining the conversation.

Eric's eyebrows shot up. "I don't know about that, I think Dani here is a bit young –"

"There's no accounting for connection. The lad's got a rhythm with the beast already. We'd best accept our good luck and take what we have," Taylor cut in.

Looking between the three faces, Eric shook his head slowly in disbelief. He was not convinced. Dani may have claimed to be nineteen but he looked closer to fifteen or sixteen to Eric. But he had ridden like a professional. Better than most professionals, Eric had to concede to himself. "Alright then," he said slowly.

Tommy let out another happy '*whoop*' and threw his arm around the younger man. "Come on, Dani! I'll let you in on all of Mercury's secrets." Tommy steered the new exercise rider back in the direction of the stables.

Taylor watched them go, keeping a firm hold on the aforementioned devil.

"If that boy is nineteen, then I'm a Classics winner already," Eric commented. Taylor laughed beside him.

"That may be. But we've still got to find a proper jockey for this beast. At least one thing is squared away." Despite the horse's terrible behavior, Taylor gave him an affectionate slap on the rump. "I am going to see this wily boy put away myself. We can talk more later if you plan on staying around."

"I don't have any engagements in town until this evening. I'll wait."

Nodding, Taylor headed in the same direction as the two exercise riders.

Eric turned back towards the track. The morning exercises had resumed now that the spectacle was over. The groom who had been leading Mercury when he got away was on his feet now, a bandage wrapped around where the headstrong horse had tried to take a bite of his upper arm.

He took a deep breath as he walked back to the rail, taking up a position several yards away from where the other trainers stood with their pocket watches out and eyes trained on the track as the horses in their charge made their morning runs. The smell of horse, manure, turf, and sweat filled his nostrils. The sweet, earthy scent reached deep into his soul.

Eric had grown up on the racecourse and in the stables. He had learned about the sport at the heels of his father and grandfather. And now the reins were firmly in his hands, so to speak. He exhaled a long, slow sigh. He prayed he had what it would take to save it for his own sons.

Chapter 2

The garden door was her best bet. There would be too many people in the kitchen; servants tended to take their breaks down there, where samples of the evening meal or unconsumed dainties might be on offer. As a young child running wild across her family estate, she had often passed an afternoon in the kitchen. Of course, their household had been small by comparison to her aunt and uncle's. In her home, everything revolved around the horses. The house was more of an afterthought. Even so, the kitchen was always a bustling place.

So, no, she could not go in through the kitchen door if she had any hope of entering the house undetected.

It was nearly dark outside. The ride had taken her longer than expected to get back to her aunt and uncle's house in Cambridge. She would have to make sure she left the stables a bit earlier. It was unlikely that anyone would look for her before six or seven o'clock in the evening when they returned from paying calls and socializing. But if they did ... well, she needed to be here. She could not risk her aunt finding out about her little deception.

And what if she did? A small voice inside of her squeaked. The worst she could do was send her back to her father in the countryside. Which was exactly what she wanted more than anything else. *Perhaps that was not the worst thing.* Her Aunt Millie would probably enjoy devising a crueler punishment.

Pushing that thought aside, she slowly turned the handle to the garden door. By some miracle it did not creak. *Excellent.* Another point in favor of the garden as her main route of egress and ingress.

She peered down into the deserted hallway. To the left was the door to the kitchen; she could hear the sounds of pots and pans at work on the stove as well as the murmur of voices. She would need to be careful of disturbing the occupants. The hallway itself was dim as she slipped inside. The gas lamps that lined the wall had not been lit yet, but someone would be along soon. Another indication that she needed to time her arrival a bit earlier or risk running into one of the footmen lighting the hallway.

Taking care to step softly, she gripped her soft muslin skirt and lifted it above her ankles so there was no chance of tripping. She made it down the hallway successfully. On her right was the servants' staircase to the upper floors. There were two more doors opposite that on the left wall; she was not sure where those went. Perhaps a pantry or wine cellar. She was fairly certain that the doorway directly ahead of her

One Race to Ruin

opened into the house's foyer. From the foyer, there were several connecting rooms: her uncle's study, the sitting room, the stairs to the next floor, and her aunt's morning room-turned sewing nook. If she appeared there, she could easily have been coming from any of those rooms. It would be quite convenient.

Much more convenient than trying to slip through the heavy front doors, which made the most onerous groan when opened. She had been fortunate to get through them undetected this morning.

The bag over her shoulder was perhaps the biggest wrinkle. There would be no need for her to be carrying it if she had just been loitering around the house. Well, she could work on a strategy for that tonight. There was nothing for it now. If she wasted any more time in this hallway, a servant was going to appear.

When she stepped into the foyer, her luck ran out.

Her aunt and uncle were coming down the stairs. *Drat, the one time she needed them to be somewhere else ...* She looked around frantically for somewhere to stash her bag.

There was a huge floral arrangement on the mirrored table against the wall. The staircase wound around the foyer in a graceful curve. In just a moment, her aunt and uncle would round the turn and she would be in view.

Without thinking twice, she shoved the bag into the blue and white delft-painted vase. Some water splashed out onto the table. She stood on her tiptoes and scooted her bum over the top of the table, feeling the water soak through her thin muslin gown, past her petticoat, and onto her leg.

"Daniela! There you are!" Her aunt exclaimed.

She forced a smile onto her face. Clasping her hands behind her back, she tried to cover her bottom as much as possible. The gown was a pale lavender muslin. She was sure that on her backside was a darker purple splotch of wetness.

"Good evening, Aunt Millie." Daniela smiled brightly. Her aunt gave her a curious look; her niece had been anything but happy since her arrival two weeks ago.

"Where have you been all day? We have hardly seen you." Millie paused to consider. *They had hardly seen her because they hadn't seen her at all*, Daniela thought to herself. But she was not going to correct her aunt.

"I spent most of the day in my rooms." She hoped the lie came off convincingly. She hadn't much practice at it. Before now, she'd never had cause to try. "I suppose I should return up there and get changed …" Daniela glanced meaningfully towards the stairs.

"Yes, you ought. I will have some food sent up for you and Winifred. I imagine we will be out quite late tonight at Lord Harker's dance." Her Aunt Millie motioned up the stairs as if dismissing her. That was just fine.

Daniela edged around her aunt and uncle as they continued into the sitting room, carefully keeping her back away from them. As soon as they disappeared, she turned and ran up the stairs as quickly as her feet could carry her. One turn at the top, another left, and she was in her room. She felt a wave of relief course through her as the door clicked shut. She leaned her forehead on it and let out a slow, restorative breath.

"Whatever has happened to your backside, Daniela?"

One Race to Ruin

Her face scrunched up instantly. Well, she was not as free as she thought. Slowly Daniela turned around, finding her younger cousin seated on the upholstered bench at the foot of her bed.

"*Dios mio*, Winnie, you gave me a fright!" Daniela decided to ignore her cousin's question. She instead walked calmly to her dressing table, sat down so the aforementioned backside was out of sight, and started taking down her hair.

"Mama says speaking Spanish is not fashionable."

"I am not exactly the fashionable type anyways." It was absurd the number of pins she had used to secure her hair. It was only as she saw the growing pile that Daniela realized it. Well, she did not want a single lock escaping. Her hair was too distinctive.

"Because you are red-haired?" Winnie looked at her sympathetically, twirling one of her own golden locks around her finger.

Daniela tried her best not to laugh. "No, Winnie. Because I do not care to *be* fashionable."

Winnie shook her head. "This is why you will never find a husband, that is what Mama says."

"Aunt Millie has a lot of useful opinions today, hasn't she?" Shaking her head, Daniela finally freed her long red locks. She reached up and massaged her scalp. *Tomorrow, fewer hairpins.*

"I hope I am not a spinster like you at nineteen." Winnie looked bereft at the thought. At seventeen years old, Winnie was the epitome of a young English rose: light blonde hair, clear porcelain skin, softly rounded figure.

"I hardly think being unmarried at nineteen qualifies me as a spinster." Daniela did not know whether to be annoyed or feel sorry for her cousin. To take everything her Aunt Millie said as gospel … it must be exhausting.

Winnie had maintained her seat on the little bench, fiddling with her fingers. Daniela hoped she would be on her way soon; she wanted to change into some dry clothes. And she needed to figure out a way to get downstairs and retrieve her bag from the vase. She would need to lay the contents out to dry …

"What are you going to wear to Lord Harker's party?" Winnie piped up.

Daniela shrugged. She hadn't given the least bit of thought to it. "I am sure you must have decided by now," Daniela said offhandedly as she started to drag her brush through her silky hair.

"I don't want to wear the same color as you."

This time Daniela did laugh out loud. "What color do you want to wear, Winnie?"

"Yellow."

"Alright then, I promise I shall not wear yellow." She wouldn't have chosen it anyway. Daniela did not know much about fashion but she did know that yellow did not compliment her coloring. Despite her Spanish heritage, she had the pale skin afforded most redheads. Her shoulders and the bridge of her nose were spattered with light freckles that one had to stand quite close to see.

Winnie finally stood up. This must have been the reason for her visit all along, Daniela realized. How odd her cousin was. Well, if it would get her on her way, well enough. Winnie looked around the room as if unsure what to do next. Daniela decided to push her along.

"Would you excuse me, Winnie? I think I'd like to have a quick bath before we go out this evening."

One Race to Ruin

"Oh," Winnie looked a little disappointed, an emotion which Daniela could not account for at all. She hardly knew her younger cousin – had only met her a handful of times before her father had sent her here a few weeks ago. And in that time, she had not gotten any closer to understanding the other young woman. "Alright then, I shall go."

"See you soon," Daniela called, continuing to brush her hair until the door closed on her cousin's retreating back. "Ooof," she let out a little sigh, sinking back in her chair. What a day. And she still had a whole night ahead of her.

For a moment, Daniela reconsidered her bath in favor of a nap. But then she caught a whiff of her own scent. No, she needed a bath. She smelled like horse.

Chapter 3

It would have been generous to call Lord Harker's party a ball. It may have been held in a ballroom – and true, he was one of the few residents of Cambridge to boast a full-size one – but the glitz and glamour of the London Season were missing. At least that was what Daniela's Aunt Millie said to her Uncle Baxter once the party arrived at the lord's expansive mansion.

It was plenty impressive to Daniela. She had certainly never attended a *proper* ball. When she arrived at her aunt and uncle's Cambridge home two weeks ago, they had just returned from London. Winnie had been presented at court, they had hosted a proper debut, and then Uncle Baxter dragged them home so that he could finish out the term at the university where he was a professor. Once the term

One Race to Ruin

ended, they would depart back to London and continue husband-hunting for Winnie full force.

Though they had adjourned to Cambridge, Daniela surmised that Aunt Millie was not going to pause in her mission. If there was a suitable man to be found in the little university town, she would find him. Hence, their attendance at the not-quite-a-ball that evening.

"Winnie, you *will not* hug the wall as you did at Lady June's last ball in London. You are not a wallflower. *Wallflowers don't win husbands*," Aunt Millie ordered her daughter as they moved further into the room. It was early yet; the ballroom was only about half full.

Daniela glanced at her cousin. Winnie had been true to her word – she wore a goldenrod yellow silk taffeta gown that practically emanated light. *Add some stripes and she would look like a bumblebee.* Daniela bit her lip and pushed down that uncharitable thought. If Winnie and her mother wanted her to attract attention they had chosen the right garment for the job.

She watched as Aunt Millie grabbed tightly onto Winnie's arm and started dragging her towards a group of similarly-aged young men and women that were chatting amiably on the other side of the room. Uncle Baxter watched them for a few seconds then turned and disappeared out the double doors of the ballroom into the hallway. Probably in search of a cigar and the library. It seemed like they had completely forgotten about Daniella's existence. Well, that suited her just fine. *She* was not in the market for a husband.

Doing exactly what her aunt had instructed Winnie not to do, Daniela backed herself up to a wall and attempted to look as unapproachable as possible. Even so, several young gentlemen gave her more than a passing look.

She needed to find somewhere other than the ballroom to hide. The longer she was in here the more likely that her aunt was to remember her existence and her promise to her brother-in-law, and force Daniela to join Winnie. Or that one of these interested gentlemen would get up the courage to try and engage her in conversation. Or worse, ask her to dance.

Keeping her eyes trained forward – the better to stare down any potential dance partners – Daniela crept along the wall. There was a door about ten yards down. Where did it go? It didn't matter; it led out of the ballroom.

There was Winnie. She was talking to a kind-looking young man; a bit rotund, with a very nice smile. Winnie appeared genuinely interested in what he was saying, smiling and laughing. And there was Aunt Millie lurking a few yards away with other matchmaking-mamas, keeping watch on the interlude. Good, they were distracted. No one would see her –

"What in Christ's name –"

"*Jesus Cristo!*"

"Are you even watching –"

"*¿Qué está haciendo –*"

Despite her attempts to keep her eyes watchful, Daniela couldn't help herself. She rounded on the man who had knocked into her, hands on her hips and disdain in her eyes.

One Race to Ruin

Her stomach dropped. Her face flushed. Her entire body started to tingle – and *not* in a good way.

"What are you doing here?" She exclaimed.

His dark eyebrows shot up in surprise. Daniela clapped her hand over her mouth.

"Excuse me?"

"I – I am so sorry. I mistook you for someone else."

"Who *do* you talk to in such a manner?"

Daniela's eyes narrowed. "That is none of your business."

"Since you are verbally assaulting me, I think it is my business." Eric crossed his arms, his eyebrows raised and a look of superior expectation on his face.

He was a huge man. Not tall though most definitely not short either. He was very solidly built: broad shoulders, heavily muscled arms that she could see even through his tailcoat. She had noted it earlier when they were at Newmarket. In his evening attire, black on black, with a stark white cravat … he looked dangerously imposing and powerful.

But Daniela was not so easily intimidated.

Once she got over the initial shock of seeing him – *Why, oh why, did he have to be here?* – she was still thoroughly annoyed at him for blocking her exit. As coincidental as it might be.

"Excuse me, sir, I –"

"My lord," he interjected.

"I'm sorry, what?"

"My correct form of address is 'my lord.'"

Daniela's mouth dropped open. The world had to be playing some kind of sick joke on her. Perhaps this was a dream and soon she would wake up in her bed from the nap she hadn't meant to take. No, this wasn't a dream. It was a nightmare.

"Excuse me, *my lord*, but I must go …" She said the address like an epithet. But as she turned to leave, the door promising her escape firmly in her sights, Daniela saw her aunt approaching. *Was this her punishment for lying to her family?*

Seeing no other course of action, she grabbed his hand.

"Quick. Dance with me. Now!" She dragged him onto the dance floor a moment before her aunt caught up with them. The music started and by complete habit Eric put one hand in hers and the other at her waist and started dancing.

"Who are you?" Eric asked, his face screwed up in a baffled, amazed, irritated grimace.

"Daniela Rames," she said, her eyes still on her aunt. Winnie and Aunt Millie stood at the edge of the dancefloor. Winnie looked distracted. She clearly wasn't interested in her cousin. But Millie was considering the dancing pair carefully.

"Rames?" Eric repeated. "Of the Cambridge Rames'? Daughter of Baxter Rames?"

"Of the Gainsborough Rames, thank you. Niece of Baxter Rames," she corrected him. Daniela watched his face as he considered.

"Gainsborough … as in Nathaniel Rames – ouch!" He cried out suddenly as she stepped hard on his foot.

Daniela grimaced. "I'm sorry. I am not much of a dancer," she admitted. She much preferred to be on horseback. But she did not voice that thought. Not to him. She didn't need to court disaster; it seemed to be finding her all on its own.

"Then why did you ask me to dance?" Eric looked down at the petite little siren in his arms with complete and utter frustration.

One Race to Ruin 23

For siren she was. She was draped in turquoise green silk that looked like she had stepped through a tropical waterfall. It fell in voluminous drapes from where it was gathered just below her breasts. The edges of the sleeves were embroidered in shiny gold thread, a little loop and swirl pattern that almost looked like a horse in motion. *Good lord, would he ever be able to escape the world of racing?* Now he was seeing horses in the embroidery of ladies' clothing!

"My aunt was approaching." She tilted her red-haired head towards the edge of the dancefloor. Eric followed her gaze, sighting the middle-aged woman who watched them with crossed arms. Her dark brown hair, liberally interspersed with gray, was in a tight chignon at the back of her head. And while she might once have been considered pretty, her skeptical frown erased all remaining traces of youthful beauty.

"She does look rather …" he searched for a word that was not offensive.

"Ha!" Daniela laughed aloud.

As she laughed, she tilted back her head, exposing the creamy skin of her throat. The long, pale expanse of her neck leading down to the suggestive swell of her breasts made something feral inside of him growl hungrily in response. Her coppery red hair came down in long curls over her back and shoulders. One wayward tendril swirled around enticingly as they danced.

While he danced, he corrected himself. One could hardly call what this young woman was doing dancing. It was more of an ungraceful bounce around the dance floor. He kept tightening his grip on her hand instinctively, applying pressure on her waist in an attempt to keep the lead. For she clearly had no idea what she was doing. Eric just managed to sidestep her next footfall.

Daniela bit her lip, a blush creeping up her cheeks as she nearly stepped on the poor man's foot yet again. *Oh, how she hated to blush.* Why must every emotion show so plainly on her face? But her pale coloring was deplorably predisposed to it.

He was watching her closely. *Did he recognize her?*

"You are the daughter of Nathaniel Rames?" Eric asked again, looking closely at her. He could see the resemblance. He'd never been introduced to the famous racehorse breeder but he had seen him at a distance.

"Yes." She nodded, looking at him curiously. "Do you know my father?"

"Only by reputation."

"Oh," Daniela breathed a little sigh of relief. Of course he would know of her father; anyone who was anyone in the world of horses in England knew her father. However, if he knew that, it would not be a far jump to connect Daniela the daughter of the famed horse-breeder to …

"Do excuse me, I must see myself to the ladies' retiring room." She broke free from his arms, walked in the opposite direction to avoid her aunt and disappeared from the ballroom. She knew there would be hell to pay when her aunt found her. Leaving a gentleman in the middle of a dance simply was not done. But Daniela could not risk it; the longer she spent with the infuriating man the closer she danced to disaster.

For a few beats of the song Eric stood dumbfounded in the middle of the dance floor. Had she really just left him standing here? It was the height of rudeness. Everyone around them had noticed; he looked quite a fool standing there amid the swirling pairs of dancers. *Oh, what did it matter?* His reputation was one scandal short of being in tatters as it was. One red-haired chit couldn't do any more damage at this point.

Shaking off the eyes of Cambridge society, he left the dance floor and headed for the door himself. He had to be up early tomorrow to see the new rider take out Mercury anyway.

Chapter 4

While the elite of London society slept away the early morning, some sixty miles away in Newmarket the racecourse and stables were already awake and buzzing. The dawn fog was just beginning to burn off, but the April morning was plenty chilly on its own.

Eric pulled his overcoat more tightly around himself, put his hands to his mouth, and blew a stream of hot air to warm them up. He'd left his gloves sitting on the table in his dressing room. Around him, horses and the staff that cared for them were moving back and forth from the training grounds. Some had already completed their morning runs. Others were prancing around excitedly.

He knew most of them. He had spent his life on this track. His father had been obsessed with horse racing. And his grandfather before him. A long line of Earls

One Race to Ruin

of Fordham had been raised at the rails of this very racecourse. That same long line of earls had slowly and almost systematically frittered away the fortune of what had once been one of the richest earldoms in England.

The cold that nipped at him now was nothing compared to the icy dread that had spread through Eric in the weeks after his father's death. It hurt desperately to lose the man who had always been his idol. Then he discovered the ruinous state of the earldom's finances. What he had always assumed to be a somewhat profitable but mostly secondary hobby had consumed the estate. What was left? Not much.

Thank god they had found this new exercise rider. Hopefully, the boy was up to the task of managing that hellion of a thoroughbred. Because Eric could not afford a single misstep or mistake. Mercury had to win and he had to win soon.

He watched Taylor approaching from the direction of the stables. Beside him walked Dani, the young man they had hired yesterday. Dani held Mercury's rein loosely but securely, looped around his arm and then clenched in his fist. *Good*, the man did not take the lessons of yesterday lightly. Once again, a queer feeling came over Eric as he watched the exercise boy. He was well dressed in the same costume as yesterday. But something was off.

As they came closer, Eric could hear Taylor giving directions.

"I want to see how he runs with a little competition. I've got Chester up on Dynasty and they'll be along in a minute. In the meantime, take him for a trot and burn off some of that energy. I want him focused when you start the run."

Dani nodded along. "What if he wants to canter, sir? He's the kind to test the rein."

"Save it for the course," Taylor instructed.

Nodding affirmatively, Dani stepped into Taylor's linked hands for a leg up and landed gracefully in the saddle. Mercury shook his great chestnut head and snorted. Leaning forward, Dani tweaked his mane and whispered something into the horse's ear. Mercury stamped his foot but otherwise seemed to accept the rider.

"Morning, sir," Taylor said, tipping his cap to Eric. Unlike last night, Eric felt no need to correct the trainer on the proper form of address for an earl. He also got the feeling that Taylor probably knew it and didn't care. Much like the young woman he had met last night.

"I've got Chester bringing Dynasty 'round –"

"I heard you telling young Dani here. Do you think Dynasty is up for it, after their little jaunt yesterday?"

"He's fit and fine. Besides, he's the only one in your stable with a chance of holding his own against Mercury." Taylor pulled out a pipe as they walked toward the rail.

Dani had taken Mercury off to the side of the track and was trotting him in large concentric circles. Eric could see the horse testing his new rider, trying to get ahold of the bit and force a faster pace. But the young man did well. He kept a tight rein, was perched adroitly over the horses' withers, his mouth moving as he spoke to the horse.

Dani did not appreciate the way that Eric was watching them – waiting for her to make a mistake. She had convinced the trainer, Taylor. But Eric, earl of whatever, remained dubious.

One Race to Ruin

She hadn't lied about her age. She was nineteen. For a boy, she might look younger. But there was nothing she could do about that. And she was more than capable of handling the horse. Beneath her, Mercury was like a spring wound tight. She could feel his eagerness to go, to run. But she kept a tight hand on his reins.

"*Guárdalo para la carrera, mi amor,*" she cooed, leaning forward over his withers. The horse seemed to like the sound of her voice so she kept talking, on and on in Spanish as they rode in circles. Eric continued to watch her.

Let him watch, she thought grumpily. Dani was finally starting to warm up, but the irritation that had been with her all morning remained.

It had been nearly one o'clock in the morning by the time the Rames family returned to their home. Daniela had to wait in her room until the household settled around her, an entire hour longer. Then she crept downstairs and removed her bag, drenched clothes and all, from the vase in the foyer. She had opened the windows of her bedroom, in hopes that a spring breeze would help dry the clothes that she had hung from a pair of hose fashioned into a drying line across two posts of her bed. But the only result had been that come the wee hours of the morning, both she and the clothes were frigidly cold.

It wasn't until she was astride Mercury that Daniela finally felt her bum start to defrost.

There was a loud neigh from the direction of the stables. Dynasty appeared with Chester already mounted. Taylor motioned them both towards the track.

"Alright, Dani boy, you're just getting the feel of him today. If he wants his head early give it to him. Don't fight him too hard. Dynasty likes to be in the front. We want to see how Mercury is going to react to that." Taylor patted the young man's leg and sent them off.

Eric crossed and uncrossed his arms as Taylor took a long draw of his pipe.

"I'm still not sure this is the best idea."

"Running him against Dynasty? We have to test him some time."

"Not that. Dani is green …" Eric watched his best hope of restoring his family fortune being ridden away by a young lad whose voice had yet to deepen.

"Green isn't always bad."

"It isn't good, either."

"He's got him in hand."

"For now."

Taylor just puffed away. Keeping the pipe poised between his lips, he pulled out his pocket watch with one hand and raised his other arm. The two horses and riders moved into position. The trainer dropped his arm and they thundered off in a churn of hooves.

Dani gave a kick and loosened the reins. Mercury needed no further encouragement. He sprang to life beneath her. He reached a full gallop in seconds, his hooves digging into the firm turf eagerly. Beside them, Dynasty was also in motion, a dark brown blur. Daniela flicked her glance over; they were half a length ahead of Dynasty. Slowly, she eased up. Having gotten out his initial burst of energy, Mercury seemed to settle in. Dynasty pulled up on his side, closing the half-length. Then they were even and then the dark bay pulled ahead.

One Race to Ruin

She could feel the moment that Mercury realized he was being passed. He dug in and lengthened his stride without her having to ask. They were ahead by half a length and then a full length. Mercury was still pulling; he had more to give, she could feel it. Then Dynasty was there challenging them again. Just as Taylor had said – Dynasty wanted the lead back.

But Mercury was not going to give it to him easily. She decided to ask him for more. Using her body and hands she urged Mercury forward and he answered. As they passed the post marking the mile they were ahead by a neck.

As both horses slowed to a canter and then a trot, their riders could be heard whooping for twenty yards in either direction. They brought them around, trotting back towards the waiting pair of trainer and owner. They were laughing and reveling as they reined in.

"It was just as you thought, sir. He did not like Dynasty trying to pass him one bit!" Dani said excitedly to Taylor.

"We might have had you if we had another furlong!" Chester said, a huge smile on his face. A groom was taking the reins for Dynasty and the exercise rider hopped down.

"Not a chance." Dani shook his head. "He had more to give. I could *feel* it."

"Could you now?" Eric stood with arms crossed, watching the revelry.

Dani cleared his through awkwardly. "Yes, my lord. He could go further. He could go faster."

"Hmmm." Eric turned to Taylor. "What do you think?"

"I think we enter him in the 2000 Guineas."

"You're sure?"

"You're not?"

"The entry fee is substantial. If he's not going to win —"

The trainer's eyebrows shot up. "With runs like that? We'll win."

Dani felt her mouth drop open. The 2000 Guineas? The Classics? *That* was what they were training Mercury for?

Eric's eyes were on Dani now. "What? You don't think he has a shot?"

"No, sir, I mean, my lord, yes, I," Dani paused, pinching herself discreetly. "Yes, my lord. I think he can. He was fast out there. And he can go faster."

Eric looked from trainer to rider and then back again. It was a huge risk. But the purse, the prestige, the breeding potential … the reward wasn't even financially quantifiable.

"Alright. The 2000 Guineas then." He nodded decisively, hoping that when the race was run in three weeks' time he would not regret it.

"Good. Here's what I have in mind for his training program …" Taylor pulled his pipe from his mouth and turned back towards the stables with Eric at his side.

Another groom had appeared to take Mercury back to the stable. Still mounted, Dani shook her head. "I'll walk him out myself, thanks." As she hopped down to the ground, bridle firmly in hand, she turned back to Mercury, whose chestnut coat was shining beautifully in the emerging morning sun.

"The 2000 Guineas," she repeated, stroking his nose. "Alright, *mi amor. Ahí vamos.*"

Chapter 5

*E*ven though it was past noon, the room where Eric sat was still heavily shadowed. He had spent the better part of two hours after Mercury and Dynasty finished their workouts talking strategy with Taylor. He could tell the man was getting irritated with him; most owners were content to let their trainer run the show so long as the stable was racking up wins. *Well, most owners did not have as much at stake as he did.*

And there had been wins. Since he had fired the incompetent man put in place by his father and handed over control of the Fordham stables to Taylor, the stable as a whole had been bringing in a steady stream of wins. And it was still early in the racing season. But Eric was on a very limited timetable. Mercury was the prize horse in his string. If he won the 2000 Guineas, that would finally give

Eric a little breathing room. It was by no means enough – not in the long term. But it would go a long way towards proving to himself that horseracing could be a profitable enterprise for the Fordham earldom. And that he wasn't as big a fool as his father and grandfather before him for risking so much on that enterprise.

Flagging down one of the liveried waiters, Eric ordered a brandy. He'd been sipping on tea long enough. He needed something stronger to calm his nerves.

As the waiter walked away, a familiar face walked through the doorway. To be fair, most of the faces here were familiar. Eric had been a member of the Jockey Club practically from birth.

But this was a face he would rather not see.

The short, pudgy man sat down in the seat across from him, with something that might technically have been a smile on his face. "Ho there, Fordham! I didn't think to see you here!"

Eric gritted his teeth. "Why not, Kenner?"

"I thought you might have given up your membership by now." Bradford Kenner waved obnoxiously. When he failed to get the attention of the waiter clearing a table on the other side of the room, he resorted to yelling. "You there! Whiskey!"

The poor young man nearly jumped out of his skin. When he saw who had hailed him, he nodded and scurried out of the room, almost spilling his tray of glassware in his haste to comply. Kenner had a certain reputation even outside of the halls of London, it would seem.

"As I said, surprised to see you here."

"And as I said, I do not know what you mean."

One Race to Ruin

Kenner leaned forward, glancing around as if they were two friends speaking in confidence. "I had heard that things were not … gainful … since the last earl passed."

Eric's pulse jumped, but he kept his face carefully neutral.

"And where did you hear such a thing, may I ask?"

"Oh, you know how it is. Everyone on the racecourse is always talking."

"Indeed. And you, of course, must listen."

The smile on Kenner's face, which had not budged, twisted into something closer to a sneer. "But of course. I would not want to be rude."

The waiter brought their drinks. Eric guessed that the two liveried young men had drawn straws to see who would have to bring the odious Kenner his beverage.

Eric thanked the man. Kenner acted as if his whiskey had appeared by magic. Swirling his drink around the snifter, Eric silently wished he had not ordered anything. Now that he was holding a full brandy he could not just get up and leave the Jockey Club Rooms.

He stared at the taupe walls, the mustard yellow velvet couch, the equine portraits that lined the walls – anything to avoid making eye contact with Kenner. But he was not going to be let off that easily.

"My trainer informed me this morning that you have entered your horse into the 2000 Guineas."

"Yes, I have."

"Feeling that confident, are you?"

"He's been making good runs."

"Good enough?"

"We think so."

"Let's hope so." Despite his red-face and flaccid appearance, Kenner put back his dram of whiskey in a single shot.

Eric was losing his patience for this conversation and its insinuations. "What do you mean by that?" He challenged.

Kenner was undeterred by his surly manner. He leaned back in his rose-upholstered chair and smiled broadly. "Come now, Fordham. Our families have long been friends."

"Our grandfathers were friends. Our fathers tolerated each other. We – are something else entirely."

"Perhaps." Kenner's dark, piggy eyes looked back at him. "Either way, let us hope that you can win the 2000 Guineas and start to make good on your father's – shall we call them," he paused emphatically, "— mistakes."

Eric said nothing. His grip on his glass had tightened so much he thought it might shatter in his hand. His knuckles were white.

Kenner looked Eric over, a look of intense satisfaction on his face. He set his glass down on the polished cherry wood table beside him and got to his feet. Ungainly as he was, it was not a graceful action. And yet, he continued to look extremely pleased with himself.

"Otherwise, we might become much more closely acquainted."

Eric's senses screamed. *What the hell did Kenner mean by that?*

He watched as Bradford Kenner licked his lips in anticipation. He wanted Eric to ask. Whatever it was that he thought he had on Eric, he wanted to lord it over him.

Determined not to give him the satisfaction, Eric lifted the brandy to his mouth and took a long drink. He kept his gaze firmly on Kenner, not allowing himself to flinch though inwardly his stomach was swirling uncomfortably.

The pompous, greasy man stared at him for several long moments more. But he seemed to realize that Eric was not going to crack. His malicious smile faded a little but he did a good job of hiding his disappointment. Clearly, he felt that whatever leverage or injury he planned to inflict, it would do as well later as now. That worried Eric immensely.

"Best of luck to you, Fordham. You shall need it."

Eric raised his glass in a silent salute but did not say anything. Kenner's eyes narrowed slightly but he did not reply further before departing.

Eric thought he saw the waiter, who stood by the doorway waiting to attend to members' needs, let out a sigh of relief when Bradford Kenner finally left the room.

He felt his own chest deflate. He sank back against the cushioned sofa where he sat, his tense grip on the snifter of brandy loosening. It was almost gone now.

What the hell had Kenner been getting at? Eric glanced at the tall grandfather clock that stood in the corner of the room. It was not too late in the day. He could still get a letter out to his solicitor by the evening post. If Bradford Kenner was somehow involved in the financial mess he had inherited, he needed to know. And he needed to know *now*.

Chapter 6

By some miracle Daniela had made it to Saturday. It had been the longest but also one of the most gratifying weeks of her life. She had developed a routine. She rose before dawn, dressed in her riding clothes, and slipped out to the stables. She rode from Cambridge to Newmarket – she could make it in an hour if she hustled. There, she would discuss the morning's exercise with Taylor, with the Earl of Fordham looking on broodingly. He had strong opinions about the horse's training; that much was clear. But beyond that first day he kept his concerns to himself. Or at least, he voiced them outside of her presence. She was just a lowly exercise rider, after all.

That suited her fine. She had not started this whole ruse to get to know the surly earl. She had gone to Newmarket dressed as a man that morning because she was desperate to reclaim some part of her identity. And riding Mercury had achieved that and more. On her father's stud farm, she had spent most of her days in the saddle. They had attended the races at Doncaster often. This was her world, but she had never seen this side of it. Because she was a woman. But when she was mounted on Mercury all things seemed possible.

After the morning exercise was over she would see Mercury walked out and settled in his stall. This was usually a groom's job, but the beast had taken a liking to her and she to him. Plus, ever since he had taken a chunk out of the groom's arm on the day they met, the stable boys and grooms had been leery.

Once Mercury was taken care of she mounted her own horse and disappeared down the road without much notice from anyone. Usually, exercise riders rode several horses in succession, for multiple stables. But Taylor hadn't batted an eye when she said she had no interest in riding for other stables. He had been happy to keep her focus on Mercury. She would ride for home, stop in a convenient grove of trees about a mile outside of Cambridge to change into her dress, and be back at her aunt and uncle's home by noon.

All in all, it was working out much more smoothly than Daniela could have hoped. But now it was Saturday. The races were on at the Rowley Mile Racecourse, and both she and Mercury would have a day of rest.

Yawning, she stretched out in her bed. She had slept late; well-deserved, she thought, after a week of early rising. Perhaps she would lay back and doze a bit more …

A sharp knock at the bedroom door brought her back to attention. "Come!" She called, sitting up in bed.

"You're still abed?" Aunt Millie herself stood in the doorway, her hands on her hips and her ever-present frown on her face. "I thought the housekeeper must be mistaken when she said you had not yet rung for a maid this morning."

"I haven't been sleeping well." So much for getting a few more minutes of respite.

"That is hardly an excuse. Get up and dressed, we will be on our way soon." Aunt Millie stepped to the side so a maid could enter the room. The maid went to the windows and started pulling the drapes under the older woman's watchful eyes.

"On our way where?" Daniela stretched and moved to stand.

"Newmarket. We are leaving in an hour. I shall expect you promptly in the hall." With a curt nod, she turned to leave.

"Newmarket?" Daniela's breath caught in her throat.

Her aunt sighed in annoyance. "Yes, Newmarket. The spring meeting is already well underway. Honestly, I would have thought for a girl who grew up on a horse farm –"

"I know what Newmarket is. I just ... why are we going?" Daniela did not roll her eyes, but it was a near thing.

"Because Baxter likes to watch the races. And all of the eligible men from the county will be in attendance." Her aunt eyed her suspiciously. "For someone who professes to love horses so dearly, you are quite hesitant ..."

One Race to Ruin

"I am just ..." Daniela paused, searching for an excuse. "Tired! As I said, I have not been sleeping well. Perhaps it would be best if I just stayed here and rested."

"Absolutely not. I –" Millie paused, an annoyed look on her face, "– your uncle promised your father we would see you introduced to society. So, you will come. I cannot countenance this resistance. You have been without a mother for too long."

Daniela's temper flared. "Yes, it is rather a shame that she died, isn't it?"

Millie pursed her lips. Daniela stared back at her, her face hard.

"As I said, we are leaving in an hour." She turned and left without further words.

Daniela punched the mattress in frustration. The last thing she needed today was to be at the racecourse. She had already met the Earl of Fordham socially once. To meet him again would be pushing her luck. It was a big racecourse, she reminded herself. And her aunt was right about one thing: in the middle of the spring meeting, the place would be packed with everyone of consequence for twenty miles. She would just have to avoid the handsome, brooding Eric, Earl of Fordham.

Resigning herself, Daniela climbed out of bed and allowed the maid to start assisting with her morning ablutions. She would put Eric from her mind – it was the best hope for her sanity.

And Aunt Millie's comment about her mother ... well, that was a wound that would never quite heal.

It had been a mistake to come by the Jockey Club Rooms this afternoon. Eric realized that as soon as he stepped inside. There were too many people who would try to engage him in conversation. And if the state of the earldom was as generally known as Bradford Kenner had implied ... well, those conversations couldn't possibly be anything other than awkward.

On a racing day, the rooms were brimming with the elite of England society. Many lords and their ladies had made the trip from London to watch the races. It was a fashionable pastime. But to gain entrance to these hallowed halls one must hold a Jockey Club membership. Sure, it could be purchased along with the ownership of a thoroughbred of any caliber. But ownership alone implied a certain level of seriousness with regard to the sport.

"Lord Fordham!"

Eric braced himself for the onslaught. He had been seen. No retreating now.

He raised his hand in greeting to Lord Bravern, who had hailed him from across the room. Making his way through the throng of people, Eric stopped a liveried waiter to order some brandy. Anything to fortify his nerves.

Before joining the group he went and poured himself a cup of tea from the service laid out on the sideboard. No cream, no sugar.

"Good afternoon, Lord Bravern. Do you have a horse running today?"

"Two! My wife would have rather stayed in London; she's not much for the races. But we've got to keep an eye on the investment!" Bravern winked broadly. A few years older than Eric at thirty, Bravern was one of the few racecourse regulars who Eric could stand.

"Where have you stashed her for now?"

"She's taking the air with her friend, Mrs. Rames. They debuted together."

"Rames?" Eric's ears perked up.

"Yes, do you know her?"

"I met a Miss Rames, recently."

"I think there is a daughter …" Bravern scrunched up his face, trying to remember.

"I think it was a cousin." Despite himself, Eric remembered Miss Daniela Rames *very* clearly.

"I haven't met the cousin. But I would assume she is here today if she is staying with them. Baxter loves the ponies," Bravern said with a laugh.

Eric was more than a little irritated at himself for the jump in his pulse. In his brief introduction to Daniela Rames, she had been singularly irritating. And she had stomped on his foot. Repeatedly.

Bravern found the Rames family of little interest. "What about you? I assume if you're here, you must have a stake in the outcomes today."

"I have entries in the first and the third," Eric confirmed.

"When is that colt of yours running? We've been hearing about him in London. Kenner says he's in fine form."

"I don't usually listen to Bradford Kenner." Even as he said the name, Eric felt his blood start to heat.

"Neither do I," Bravern wrinkled his nose in distaste.

"I've entered Mercury in the 2000 Guineas." Eric accepted the brandy the waiter delivered, putting aside his cup of tea.

Bravern's eyebrows raised but his look was respectful rather than derisive. "He is as good as they are saying."

Eric felt a little surge of affection for Bravern. Perhaps he ought to count the man among his friends. "We certainly hope so."

A look of something resembling pity entered Bravern's eyes. "I hope so too, my friend."

The creeping unease that had lingered in Eric's stomach for days started to move through his veins more definitively. *So it was known*. Despite his efforts to keep things quiet, the earldom's faltering state had become public knowledge. Eric gritted his teeth.

It didn't change anything, Eric told himself. The stakes were the same.

"If you'll excuse me, Bravern, I need to go speak to my trainer." He tossed back the remainder of his brandy, handed it to a passing waiter, and left as quickly as was dignified.

Well-dressed patrons walked along the pathways and manicured lawns outside of The Jockey Club Rooms, some women holding parasols against the early spring sun. Eric tried to keep his head down. He did not want to talk to anyone. He made one right turn, and then another, hardly noticing where he was going.

When he looked up he found himself at the fenced paddock where the pony riders left their mounts. The walk to and from the barns and stables was long; if a rider needed to find food or use the necessaries, they had to have somewhere to tie up their mount.

Sighing, Eric walked over and leaned against the fence, resting his boot on the lower rung. He held out his hand and one of the pony horses trotted over, nuzzling him in search of snacks. Pony horses were by necessity calmer and friendlier than the high-strung thoroughbreds they were charged with escorting to and from the racecourse.

Discovering he had no food to offer, the sorrel gelding shook his head and then trotted off in the opposite direction. Eric following him with his eyes. On the other side of the paddock a small string of horses had congregated in one area. Eric walked slowly along the fence so he could get a better view. *It was a woman*, he realized.

No, it was *the* woman.

She was petite but perfectly formed, he could tell even from a distance. And he remembered quite clearly how she'd felt in his arms. Her distinctive red-gold hair was pinned back, but the curls fought their restraints. He could see springs of silky chestnut curving around her face. Did she have freckles to match? Eric imagined slipping his fingers beneath the neckline of her gown and sliding it off her shoulder to have a closer look.

Without thinking about his actions, his feet carried him in long strides around the paddock.

"You seem to get on with horses better than you do with people," he observed drolly.

Daniela jumped, upsetting the horse who was eating out of her hand and causing him to paw at the ground and step backward. She recognized the voice instantly. Worry snaked through her – *this was just the man she was supposed to be avoiding*! – joined by something else she could not quite identify. Anticipation, maybe? And why would seeing Lord Fordham cause her to feel *that*?

She straightened herself and then stretched her hand out again. "I find that horses are superiorly intelligent to most people I meet." There was grain in her outstretched hand and her equine companions returned to her eagerly.

"I cannot help but agree with you on that observation." A small chuckle escaped.

Daniela felt her lips curve naturally in response. She chanced a glance over at him. The Earl of Fordham was a handsome man. A huge brooding brute of a man, but handsome.

"Well, it seems we can agree on something other than my lack of skill on the dance floor." She should leave; make an excuse and beat a hasty retreat back to the safety of her family. But she could not quite bring herself to disengage from the conversation.

"Dancing as a pastime is overrated."

"Another thing on which we heartily agree." She felt her heart starting to beat more rapidly. He was standing a full three feet away from her, leaning against the paddock fence casually.

Although she had seen Eric every day for a week, she had never seen him like this. At the track, talking strategy with Taylor, he hardly paid Dani the exercise rider any attention. But the look on his face now as he spoke to Daniela the woman ... made an unfamiliar, tingling warmth rush through her. Despite the coolness of the spring day, she felt like the air was pressing in around her.

"I would expect to have a great deal in common with the daughter of the most well-known horse breeder in England, given both of our upbringings."

Daniela felt her chest tighten at the mention of her father. "I'm afraid you have me at a disadvantage, my lord. You seem to know so much about me, and yet I know so little about your background."

"Eric Weathers, Earl of Fordham." He bowed as he introduced himself. Of course, she knew exactly who he was. But she couldn't let on and risk exposing her deception.

"Fordham? You are right; we have more in common than I initially thought."

"Both the children of the racing obsessed."

"And perhaps both racing obsessed ourselves?" She cocked one of those chestnut red eyebrows and Eric felt a little lurch inside of him. He resisted the urge to reach out and trace his finger along that delicately arched brow; it was a ludicrous thought.

Daniela's second eyebrow raised to match the first as she looked at him questioningly. He cleared his throat awkwardly. "I can only speak for myself. I am deeply involved in managing the stables I inherited from my father."

"Well, I am not involved, at the moment. Obviously, because I am in Cambridge rather than Gainsborough." Her voice was tinged with bitterness. *Get ahold of yourself*, she reprimanded herself. Instead of staying away from the man, she was pouring out her heart to him.

"And yet you still find yourself at the racecourse."

"My Uncle Baxter enjoys the races."

"You could have remained in the grandstand."

"I could have. But as you said, I prefer the company of horses to people."

She seemed bothered by something – the mention of her father, maybe. Eric felt an unexplainable urge to put his arms around her and comfort her. He imagined resting his chin on top of her bright red hair and breathing in the scent of her.

As fast as the image came to his mind, he shoved it away, horrified. How could he possibly be thinking about such things, with the very existence of his family estate at stake? He could not afford this kind of distraction. He could not afford *any* distraction.

"I must go. I have a horse entered in the first race." Eric started to go but then turned back to Daniela. "May I escort you to the rail to watch, Miss Rames?"

Daniela hesitated. Eric did not seem entirely sure of the action himself; he was watching her with an inscrutable look upon his face. Well, if he hadn't recognized her by now, perhaps he wasn't going to. And he was certainly superior company to her aunt, uncle, or cousin.

"Very well," she nodded and slid her hand into his proffered one. He took her delicate fingers into his own, surprised by the strength with which she gripped his. *Did she ride herself?* He wondered as he felt the callouses on her palms. Almost as if she was used to holding reins in her hands.

As he led her around the paddock and back out towards the course itself, Daniela was struck by big he was. She was used to seeing him from atop Mercury's back. At seventeen hands tall, Mercury was tall for a thoroughbred. Much like his owner, he was thickly muscled with a strong, broad chest. However, while Mercury's chestnut coat mirrored her bright locks, Eric's hair was a dark, inky black that shone with an almost violet sheen in the filtered sunlight.

He glanced over at her and saw her eyes on him. Daniela blushed.

One Race to Ruin

Eric looked away quickly, knowing from the way she stiffened that he had made her uncomfortable. A distraction was certainly in order.

"What brings you to Cambridge, Miss Rames?"

Daniela was grateful for the diversion. "My aunt and uncle live here. You said you were acquainted with my uncle, Baxter Rames?"

"Yes, he's a professor at the University of Cambridge, but he spends a great deal of his time here at Newmarket."

"I did not know that until recently," Daniela mumbled under her breath. Eric wondered at her tone but didn't question it when she continued speaking. "I expected we would be spending most of our time in London since my cousin Winnie is debuting this season."

"Ah yes, that is what Bravern meant."

"Bravern?"

"A friend of mine. He mentioned a daughter in the Rames family, but I did not think he was speaking of you." A new question entered Eric's mind. "You said your cousin's debut season ... not yours?"

Daniela made a sound somewhere between a derisive laugh and a snort. "I have no desire to be launched on London society."

"And yet you were disappointed to return to Cambridge?"

She shook her head, the bright red-gold catching the sunlight. It was brighter than a chestnut, softer ... *good lord, was he comparing her to a horse again?* Eric admonished himself internally.

"Cambridge is fine," Daniela shrugged. "It is all the same to me. I just need to make it to the end of the season and then I am going home."

"Back to Gainsborough?"

"Yes." She nodded her head definitively as if punctuating the word with her physical motion. They were nearing the Rowley Mile. The crowd had thickened as people vied for a spot at the rail. The race would start eight furlongs back. There were spectators spread out all along the course. But the prime spots were near the finish line.

Eric steered them expertly through the crowd, making further conversation impossible. Daniela let out a little breath she did not realize she had been holding. The conversation was undoubtedly about to turn to her father and his farm. And that was not a topic she wanted to broach with anyone just now. Not until she had word from her father that things had calmed down.

Maneuvering through the throng of well-dressed men and women, Eric managed to reach the rail where his trainer, Taylor, waited with a groom.

"Thank you for holding the spot," Eric thanked the groom, who sidled out of the way to make space at the rail for the Earl of Fordham. The man tipped his hat and then disappeared through the crowd. Daniela watched him disappear with a little smile; she had spoken with that groom every day for the past week after workouts and he had not even batted an eye upon seeing her today. Her ruse was working unexpectedly well.

"Mr. Taylor, allow me to introduce Miss Rames." Eric motioned towards Daniela. Taylor looked only vaguely interested. His eyes piqued at her name, and he gave her another look.

"Any relation to Nathaniel Rames?" He asked.

One Race to Ruin 51

"He is my father," Daniela confirmed. She was not surprised when Taylor did not take her hand or greet her formally. In her experience, most horse trainers had very little interaction with society women and even less with those considered debutantes. She bristled internally at her own characterization.

Taylor gave her a considering look before saying: "Rames is a good man. Despite what anyone might say." Then he turned back to the track.

Daniela's heart gave an uncomfortable lurch. She saw the look of confusion on Eric's face but she determinedly ignored it. She moved closer to the rail, into the space that Eric had cleared for her.

She scrutinized the contenders as their jockeys rode them up the track and then back down towards the starting line. "Dynasty shouldn't have any competition," she said to herself.

"This should be a relatively easy run for him, barring any major incidents," Eric agreed. Then his brow furrowed. "How did you know Dynasty was my entry?"

"I previewed the program for today," Daniela said quickly, keeping her eyes down. If she looked at Eric directly, she was sure he would see her creeping blush and the falsehood in her face. "And I overheard my Uncle Baxter speaking with an acquaintance and placing bets when we first arrived." She hoped that sounded plausible enough.

In any event, Eric was not able to question her further. The race was about to begin. In the distance they could see the horses being lined up in their post positions. There was a moment of silence; it was Eric's favorite part of the entire day. In the seconds before the flag dropped and the horses thundered down the track, it was as if the entire crowd took a deep inhale and held their breath.

Then the starter's flag fell and they were off. All around them spectators watched eagerly, vying to see over one another's heads.

The jockey aboard Dynasty wore royal blue silks with a simplified golden eagle upon them, an homage to the Earl of Fordham's family crest. Dynasty liked to be at the front. As the horses came close enough to distinguish, it was easy to see the blue of the silks against Dynasty's dark coat at the lead.

Daniela's heart was racing, just as it did during every race she had ever watched. She had never had a stake in the race. Her father bred horses; he didn't race them. But she found that her stomach was in knots, her heart rooting for Dynasty to hold his place at the front. She leaned forward against the rail, instinctively trying to get as close as she could to the action. Her body pressed up against Eric's hand.

Glancing down, Daniela saw that he gripped the rail tightly, his knuckles white with tension. She felt the strangest urge to cover his hand with her own, to join their hopes and anticipation. *Of course, that was out of the question.* She was pushing her luck just being down here with him, both of them unmarried, without an escort from her family.

All of these thoughts raced through her head. But as the horses thundered towards the finish line, her mind cleared of everything but the race.

Dynasty was ahead by half a length. She watched as the jockey glanced over his shoulder – a challenger was coming up on their left flank. The jockey leaned forward and asked Dynasty for more. The horse gave

One Race to Ruin 53

it, sprinting forward and stretching his lead to a full length as he pounded past the finish line.

Daniela let out a little '*whoop*' of excitement. Without realizing it, she grabbed Eric's hand on the rail just as she had envisioned. A relieved chuckle bubbled out of Eric's chest. Taylor was nodding repeatedly, a satisfied smile on his face.

The crowd immediately began to thin and Eric and Daniela came back down to reality. Eric looked down at their hands, his eyebrows flying upwards towards his hairline. Daniela's mouth opened into a surprised little 'o.' She pulled her hand back, clasping them both in front of her, her knuckles now the white ones.

She had no idea what had come over her. Not trusting herself or her traitorous body at all, Daniela took a step back into the clearing space behind her. Although she was sure her cheeks burned red and she wanted nothing more than to run away in embarrassment, she forced herself to smile. "Congratulations, my lord. It was very well run."

Eric felt his breath coming in hot waves. *What had just happened?* The last minute was a muddle in his mind: a blur of racing pulse, racing horses, heat from the crush of people around them, heat from her hand on his at the rail. It was more than his addled mind could process.

"Thank you," he managed to say. Taylor was already heading towards the knot of people gathering around the winning horse and jockey, expecting Eric to follow him. Eric opened his mouth to excuse himself but Daniela beat him to it.

"I must find my family. They will be wondering where I have gotten to." She curtsied – *Why? She had no idea* – and started to move away and put some distance between them. "Thank you for the diversion, Lord Fordham."

Before she could make another gaffe, Daniela turned and retreated in search of her aunt and uncle. She could not help laughing at herself – *retreating to her Aunt Millie for respite? What an outlandish thought!*

Chapter 7

"Well, it has been a good run. But it looks like this devil beast is determined to keep himself out of the 2000 Guineas if it takes his dying breath." Eric brought his fist down hard on the railing, then turned around and stalked off in the opposite direction.

Taylor did not bat an eye. He took another puff of his pipe and watched as the groom caught Mercury's bridle and wrestled him back in the direction of the stables. Dani cringed; the poor man was going to get the worse end of that altercation. She pushed away from the rail to go intervene.

"Let it be, lad."

Dani froze at Taylor's voice. She looked after the pair, horse and groom, but did as the trainer bid.

They had tried out four jockeys on Mercury in the past week. The horse had thrown off one, refused to run beyond a canter for another, caught the bit in his teeth and taken off like a wild thing down the Newmarket Heath training gallop with the third barely hanging on aboard, and tried to take a nibble off the fourth.

Despite herself, Dani was starting to agree with Eric. If they couldn't find a jockey to ride Mercury in the first of the Classics, then it did not matter how fast his trial runs were.

"What do you think we are missing?" Taylor asked, sparing a glance over at Dani.

Dani's eyebrows shot up. Trainers and owners did not usually consult with their exercise riders; they usually just gave them direction. But Mercury was a special case. And they were all running out of ideas.

She considered the question, cocking her head to one side. "He wants a rider who respects him."

"I wouldn't even put up a jockey who I knew didn't respect my horses," Eric said. He stood a few feet behind Taylor and Dani, his arms crossed against his chest and a look of consternation on his face.

Dani tried not to bristle at his tone. "Of course, *my lord*," she could not help emphasizing the honorific with a hint of sarcasm. "He needs someone who can read when he needs to be pushed and will push him. It's an instinct."

"That's very helpful."

"You asked my opinion –"

"Taylor asked –"

"That's enough, children." Taylor intervened, blowing a circle of smoke out after a long drag on his pipe. "Since Tommy is off in Yorkshire, Dani here is the best authority we have on managing that horse."

One Race to Ruin 57

Taylor ignored Eric rolling his eyes. Dani did not. She shrugged her shoulders and made a little sound of irritation. "The 2000 Guineas is two weeks away. We are running out of time to find a jockey and give them time to adjust to each other."

Eric made a sound that might have been a sigh or a groan of frustration. He turned to Dani. "Do you have someone in mind?"

Dani chewed her bottom lip. She enjoyed watching the haughty Earl of Fordham squirm. She knew he did not like having his knowledge questioned. Would it be different, this conversation, if he knew who he was really speaking to? She was a woman, so maybe not. But he had been impressed and respected her thoughts when they had spoken on race day last Saturday. So, maybe yes.

"Do you know Tatum Greene?"

"He's retired," Eric said automatically. "Besides, he's based out of Doncaster."

"Not anymore. He moved to Bury St. Edmunds last year to be closer to his daughter and her children," Dani put in.

"Greene ... that is a thought," Taylor mused. He snuffed out his pipe, emptied the ashes onto the turf, and then tucked it into its leather wrapping inside his breast pocket.

"He's retired," Eric repeated.

"Everyone has a price." Taylor was taking hold of the idea, Dani could see.

"He is a friend of –" She caught herself just before she said it: *a friend of my father's*. If she contacted Greene, she knew he would come in a minute. But she could not go to him, not as herself. "I met him once or twice in Doncaster." She trained her eyes down.

"Assuming we could convince him to come, there is no telling how he would get on with Mercury. We still have a few options here …" Eric trailed off. He could see the look on Taylor's face. Eric knew he was beaten. "Alright. Do you have his address?" He looked to Dani expectantly.

"Not exactly. But he shouldn't be too hard to find. Bury St. Edmunds is not that big, from what I understand."

"Fine. We'll go today." Eric started walking away.

"We, sir?" Dani gulped.

"Is that a problem, Dani?" Eric turned back around, his face screwed up with annoyance. At just that moment, he seemed huge. Meeting him like this from the ground, dressed as a young man, Dani felt a wave of intimidation wash through her.

"No, sir. I just need a moment to send off a message, if I may," she squeaked.

"Fine. I will meet you on the road in fifteen minutes." With that, Eric stalked off.

Beside her, Taylor let out a chuckle. "You keep him on his toes, don't you, lad?" Without waiting for an answer, he padded after Eric.

Well, damn. Dani glanced upwards at the sky; it was almost midday. She had already stayed longer in Newmarket than she ought to. It would take a rider a solid hour to reach her uncle's home and deliver a message on her behalf. Well, she didn't have much of a choice. She would have to find someone willing – *thankfully she had a small coin purse in her bag* – and come up with a good excuse to tell her aunt.

One Race to Ruin

In the end, the note Daniela sent her aunt said she had been visiting a friend at the racecourse and had been invited back to their home for tea. It was painfully vague and thin as far as excuses went, and Daniela guessed her aunt would be less than pleased at her when she did eventually arrive home. But she did not see any other way out of her predicament.

She did manage to find a few minutes alone in the hayloft to take off her cap and re-pin her hair. After riding Mercury for his morning run and arguing with the Earl of Fordham, the long red curls were dangerously loose.

Now they were mounted, having ridden out from Newmarket towards Bury St. Edmunds. Eric rode an impressive black thoroughbred whose coat matched his rider's hair. When they had first emerged from the stable yard, the sight of them had taken Dani's breath away. Eric sat his horse with style and grace that one would not have expected from a man of his size and build. As they rode along the lane, she quietly observed him. He held the reins with casual confidence. He was clearly at home in the saddle. He asked his mount to trot, canter, and then walk with almost imperceptible cues. It was obvious to Dani that this was his horse; not one he had merely chosen for the ride from the many in his Newmarket stables.

Meanwhile, Dani was riding a very serviceable bay horse that acted most of the time as a stablemate to the needier and high-strung horses. A sturdy fellow, but not the kind of ride that Dani was watching Eric enjoy.

As they approached the outskirts of the village they slowed their horses to a walk.

"He's a thoroughbred, but I haven't seen him out for runs," Dani ventured once they were close enough to hear one another.

Eric glanced over at her as if surprised that Dani had spoken. She felt a prickle of irritation. Was the Earl of Fordham so arrogant that he looked down on making conversation with an exercise rider?

But Eric spoke without consternation. "Cerberus was bred to be a runner. Everything in his bloodlines suggested that he ought to be quite formidable at the stayers' distance. But alas —"

"Sometimes breeding only goes so far," Dani finished knowingly.

"Precisely. But he's an excellent ride. My father gifted him to me a few years ago for my twenty-fifth birthday."

"That's quite an extravagant gift." Dani felt proud of that comment. Of course, Daniela had been gifted her first horse at the young age of five. But Dani the exercise boy would have naturally come from more modest means. No one had asked her about Dani's background, but she had a story ready.

"He wasn't making any money on the track. Honestly, I think my father was happy to unload him." *If only he had been so prudent with the rest of his management of the estate*, Eric couldn't help thinking.

Dani saw the cloud pass over his face and wondered at it. "Have you thought of breeding him?" She asked, trying to divert the conversation.

"I have not. As I said, he wasn't much of a racer."

One Race to Ruin

"Fair enough. But sometimes it will skip a generation. The foals he sires could be the next Gold Cup winners."

Eric considered that. "You have quite a bit of knowledge for someone of your ... background?" Though in all honesty, Eric knew nothing about the young man's background.

Dani cleared her throat, trying to make the sound coming out of her gravelly and masculine. "Mother worked as a governess. She taught all of us to read the same books as her charges and to talk proper. We were fortunate. My father is the one who is interested in racing. Used to read us the racing forms as our bedtime stories."

Eric chuckled. "It doesn't sound unlike my upbringing."

They were fully into the village now and as the lane turned it opened onto what was obviously the high street. "It looks like there is a post office down that way." Eric nodded his head towards the northern end of the street. "Let's stop in and ask after Greene's address."

He used the time inside the post office to recompose himself. He had the oddest feeling in the pit of his stomach. There was something damnably familiar about Dani. He rode exceptionally, even on the unremarkable gelding he'd been allocated for this errand. But of course, he rode exceptionally. That was why they had hired him as Mercury's exercise rider in the first place.

But there was something about the way the young man tilted his head, pushing his chin out pugnaciously, that rang eerily familiar ...

"May I help you, my lord?" A stout, middle-aged man appeared behind the polished countertop.

"I am looking for the residence of Mr. Tatum Greene."

The post officer looked at Eric appraisingly but did not immediately answer.

"I believe Mr. Greene is resident in these parts?" Eric rephrased his request.

"Aye, you've the right of it," the man nodded, his hand coming up to scratch his salt and pepper stubbled chin. "Mr. Greene is a private man. He doesn't much like to be disturbed."

Eric nearly laughed at the ridiculousness of it. He had ridden an hour out of his way to try and convince a washed-up jockey to ride a horse that might be the devil incarnate but who was also his best chance of righting his family fortunes. And now he was being tripped up by a village postmaster.

"I appreciate your diligence, sir. I am interested in hiring Mr. Greene to ride a horse –"

"Mr. Greene is retired."

"I understand that, but –"

"What is taking so long?" Dani said impudently as she opened the door. The Earl of Fordham looked very annoyed. And the postmaster across the countertop looked very stubborn.

"This man refuses to give me Mr. Greene's address." Eric could not believe this was happening. He reached into the breast pocket of his coat and started removing coins, putting each down on the counter with a loud *clink*.

The gruff postmaster watched him put down the money. Then he reached his hand out, covered the

One Race to Ruin

coins, and slid them back across the counter towards Eric.

Dani stepped in before Eric could lose his temper completely. "Good sir, I am a friend of Mr. Greene's. We were acquainted at Doncaster —"

"Everyone at Doncaster was acquainted with Mr. Greene."

"Yes, sir, rightly so. We don't mean to harass the man," Dani glanced meaningfully back at Eric then leaned forward across the counter, speaking conspiratorially. "Don't mind the lord, you know how they are, sir." Dani heard Eric growl behind her, but she ignored it. "My mam was friends with Mr. Greene's late wife, Agatha. We've just come to ask him a bit of a favor, the families being old friends."

She spoke low, praying that Eric would not hear her. In truth, her father and Greene *were* old friends and she had no doubt that if she came to Tatum as Daniela Rames, he would have denied her very little. But as Dani the exercise rider, trying to avoid the Earl of Fordham's suspicion, this was proving to be much trickier.

"A friend of Agatha's, eh?" The man uncrossed his arms, leaning forward on the countertop as well. He still did not look entirely convinced but his loosened posture gave Dani all the encouragement she needed. She'd grown up with only her father and the staff on the farm as companions. She was as comfortable talking to so-called commoners as she was to the upper-class nobility of whom her aunt and uncle considered themselves a part. As she spoke she was picturing a stable hand named Henry who had been of an age with her. She tried to channel his mannerisms and verbiage.

"Aye, Aggie was a great friend of my mam's. It's a pity they didn't move down here sooner to be closer to Nelle and all those wee ones, while she was still alive." It *was* a pity, and something that Tatum greatly regretted. And it rang true with the postmaster.

"You've got the right of that, sure enough, lad." He stood up, not quite smiling but also much more open. He darted a look at Eric, who stood dumbfounded by the door. "Mr. Greene lives off of the Old Mill road. About a quarter-mile out of town on the high street, and then left. There's a blackberry bramble; the road cuts right through it. You'll find his daughter's farm and his cottage at the end of the lane."

"Thank ye kindly, sir." Dani tipped her hat politely. She scooped Eric's coins into her hand, flicking one back to the postmaster with a wink. The man caught it and winked back. Then she headed out the door, knowing that Eric would follow her.

"What did you say to him?" Eric demanded.

"Folks don't always appreciate being intimidated, sir." Dani used the address just to rile him. "Here." She held out her hand to return the pile of coins.

Eric opened his palm. As Dani slid the coins into his hand, her fingertips grazed his palm. Her breath caught in her throat. She looked up at him quickly, her gaze caught in his. His eyes were blue. Not bright or intense; soft, like cornflower. How could she possibly think of him as soft? He was all muscle and brawn ...

His hand closed over the coins and he stepped away abruptly, mounting up on his horse. Dani stood there awkwardly for a moment, feeling disappointed. *Don't be daft, you are dressed as a boy,* she reminded herself. She quickly turned back to her horse and mounted as well, hoping that the Earl of Fordham had not noticed his exercise rider staring up into his eyes romantically. *Good lord, would this day ever end?*

Chapter 8

"Maybe you should let me do the talking."

"Aren't I the one who is going to pay the man to come out of retirement?"

"Yes, but things did not go so well in town …"

"I think I can manage this. I have spent my entire life around jockeys." Eric knocked on the door before Dani could speak again. He was beginning to regret bringing the young man along. He was far too self-confident for a boy whose voice still cracked.

"Hello, the house!" Dani bellowed. Eric shot him an exasperated look but Dani did not cower.

A petite, well-rounded woman opened the door. She must have been in her late forties or fifties, from the gray patina of hair that was visible beneath her neatly pinned white cap. Her eyes widened when they landed on Eric. He stood as tall as the cottage's doorway. "Good afternoon, sir," she said, bobbing a curtsey.

Eric did not mince words. "We are looking for Mr. Tatum Greene. Is he at home?"

"Aye, sir, he is." She noticed Dani, who stood a couple of feet behind Eric. They must have looked an odd pair. "I am Mrs. Rivers, the housekeeper. May I ask who is calling?"

"Eric Weathers, Earl of Fordham and my ..." Eric shrugged his shoulders – "exercise boy."

"An earl and an exercise boy?" She repeated as if she had not heard Eric correctly.

"Sounds like a comedy skit, doesn't it, ma'am?" Dani piped in. Mrs. Rivers rewarded Dani with a smile and a laugh, clearly put at ease.

"It does at that, young man. If you'll come along, my lord, I can take you to the parlor while I find Mr. Greene." She looked under Eric's arm – for she certainly could not have seen over his shoulder – at Dani. "Will your young man be accompanying you?"

"I suppose he must," Eric said, rolling his eyes.

Mrs. Rivers escorted them into the cottage, settling them into a tidy little parlor that faced the front of the house. It was modest but well kept. The furniture was in good condition and comfortable. Several paintings of horses hung on the walls. Both Dani and Eric recognized the portraits, though they said nothing to each other: they were of famous thoroughbreds which Greene had ridden to victory in the Classics during his storied career.

"You know Mr. Greene." Eric stated it as fact, not a question.

Dani froze in front of the portrait of Denver Driver, the chestnut colt that Greene had ridden to victory in the 2000 Guineas back in '23.

"You suggested him for the post and you said something of a personal nature to the postmaster which convinced him to grant us Mr. Greene's direction." Eric was looking at her expectantly, waiting for an explanation.

Perhaps I'm just cleverer than you. Dani bit back the retort. If she got too mouthy the Earl of Fordham would know she was up to something for sure.

"My mam was friends with his wife." Dani decided to repeat the lie she had told the postmaster. If she said that she personally knew Greene and then the man showed up and did not recognize Dani the exercise boy, she would not be able to talk her way out of that. And right now she was busy praying that Tatum did not recognize her as Daniela Rames, daughter of his longtime friend Nathaniel.

"Was?" Eric questioned astutely.

"Mrs. Greene passed on a few years back. I've never met Mr. Greene myself, sir." Dani watched Eric closely as she spoke, hoping he was buying it.

He furrowed his brow, his thick, dark eyebrows coming closer together over his pale blue eyes. *Was his hair as soft as it looked?* Daniela wondered. *Oh, bother, keep focused!* She chastised herself.

Eric seemed to be satisfied with her explanation. "Well, let's hope we don't need to tread on the strength of that family connection to win Mr. Greene to our cause."

Mrs. Rivers reappeared in the doorway to the parlor. "I do apologize for the inconvenience, my lord, but Mr. Greene has said he is too occupied to

One Race to Ruin 69

step away at the moment. If you would like to come back another time –"

"Our matter is rather urgent, I'm afraid." Eric was done being held up at every turn. This task needed to be accomplished, and now.

"He's in the stable, my lord. I don't know how long …" She trailed off as Eric strode past her towards the back of the house.

Shocked herself, Dani mumbled an apology and jogged after him, outpaced by his significantly longer gait.

It was easy enough to find the stables. The little building stood between Greene's cottage and the slightly larger house a hundred yards away. On some plane of consciousness, Eric thought that must be the home of Greene's daughter since that was the supposed reason for his relocation to Bury St. Edmunds. But his only conscious thoughts were of finding the man and browbeating him into joining their cause.

"Por el amor de Dios, hombre terco."

Eric heard Dani muttering something unintelligible behind him. *Was that Spanish?* Then he was striding into the little stable and coming to an abrupt halt.

"Mr. Greene, I am thrilled to finally make your acquaintance." Eric stuck out his hand to the slight, grizzled man before him.

Tatum Greene looked thoroughly unimpressed. Dani slid to a halt just behind Eric. Greene flicked his eyes over the newcomer, and finding nothing of interest, turned them back to Eric. Dani let out a sigh of relief.

"I am the Earl of Fordham. I think you knew my father –"

"Aye, I knew him. A right fool." With that condemnation Greene turned back to the horse he had been attending to, a pretty sorrel mare, bringing a brush down over her neck in a familiar and repetitive motion.

Eric bit his lip to keep the retort from coming out. It cost him, but instead he said: "You are not wrong, sir."

Greene had not been expecting to hear that. He turned back to Eric and crossed his arms, brush still in hand. "Does it run in the family?"

"I certainly hope not."

"Why have you come? I am not involved in racing anymore."

"I find myself in need of a jockey."

Greene made a derisive sound. "So, foolishness is hereditary." He turned back to the horse.

"I insist you hear what I have to say," Eric said firmly, not backing down.

"From what I hear, the Earl of Fordham is not in much of a position to insist on anything."

That piqued Dani's interest. She stepped forward so she could hear everything clearly, though she remained completely unnoticed by either man.

"You've heard correctly." It hurt to say. But there was nothing else for it; Eric was running out of time to bring a jockey on board for Mercury and he'd already wasted half a day pursuing Greene. But seeing those portraits in Greene's parlor had reminded him of just how skilled a jockey the man had been, and hopefully still was. Eric could not afford for this to be a fruitless endeavor.

One Race to Ruin

"The 2000 Guineas will either be the beginning of rebuilding or the last hurrah for my family's long career as racehorse owners. You've heard correctly, and my father was a fool, at least when it came to managing the financial side of racing."

Dani almost gasped aloud, but she managed to contain herself. No wonder the Earl of Fordham was so surly. This was not just another race and Mercury was not just another horse. The stakes were high. That was a situation that Dani had the misfortune of being intimately familiar with.

The retired jockey's face was inscrutable but Eric kept talking. "But this horse is not ordinary. Mercury can win this if we can find him the right rider. He has what it takes; not just to win the 2000 Guineas, but all of the Classics. Jackson Taylor has taken him on to train him."

The change in Greene's face was subtle but Eric thought he could see the softening around the man's eyes. Taylor was well known and respected as a trainer all across Britain.

"Taylor would not have entered him in the 2000 Guineas if he did not think he could win," Greene allowed.

"You're right about that. We are not willing to compromise on Mercury. He must have the right jockey aboard if he's to meet his potential."

"And what makes you think I am that jockey? I am retired," Greene reminded Eric.

"I saw you ride at Doncaster once, sir," Dani piped in. Both men turned around and looked at her as if they had forgotten she existed.

"Mercury's exercise rider, Dani," Eric said by way of introduction. He was not sure what the young man had to add, but at this point he was ready to accept any help offered.

"I saw you ride to the win aboard Denver Driver at Doncaster in '23," Dani said.

"A lot of people saw me in that race, lad. What's your point?"

"You didn't even lay a hand on him. You asked, he gave, you barely touched the reins. You just *knew* how to get him to run. That's the kind of rider Mercury needs."

Despite himself, Eric could not help but find himself impressed by Dani's eloquence.

Greene did not appear as impressed. He snorted, then turned back and resumed brushing the horse, who had been standing there patiently while the three of them carried on.

Eric and Dani exchanged glances. What else was there to do? Eric steeled himself. He would pull out his pocketbook if he must, if it really was a matter of money. He had put so much into this endeavor already; a last-ditch investment was not going to hurt him anymore.

"Alright."

A grin spread across Dani's face. Eric turned back to Greene. "Thank you, Mr. Greene –"

"I will take the horse out for a ride. Then we'll see," Greene clarified.

Eric did his best to look circumspect, but Dani could not wipe the grin off of her face. Once he was aboard Mercury, felt what he could do, he would not be able to walk away. She was certain of it.

"That is very reasonable, sir." Eric shook the man's hand. "We are training at Newmarket, of course.

We'll be on the Newmarket Heath training gallop tomorrow morning."

"Fine, fine, I will be there tomorrow. I remember how it goes. Now get on about your business. This horse won't put herself away." Greene nodded at Dani and then turned back to the mare, thoroughly and effectively dismissing them.

Eric retreated from the stable without a word, but he wore a look of self-satisfaction on his face. Dani followed behind him as he walked the long way around the side of the house back towards their mounts waiting in front of the cottage.

Despite herself, she could not quiet the thrill of attraction that was beating through her. It was distinctly *arousing* to see Eric take charge of the situation. Especially when it was not directed at her. This growing attraction to the Earl of Fordham was very unsettling. Especially when she was garbed in breeches and her breasts bound. She climbed back into the saddle and set off behind him for Newmarket, thankful for the brisk pace that prevented further disquieting conversation.

Chapter 9

She struggled over the last few lines of her letter. She did not want her father to worry – *Lord knew*, he had enough to be worried about these days without adding her to the list. But she also did not want to give him the impression that she was too comfortable here. Daniela's worst-case scenario was that the end of the season would come, and instead of sending her home to her father, she would be trapped in Cambridge indefinitely. *Well, almost her worst-case scenario.*

Sighing, she decided to say no more. She folded the paper carefully, applied her uncle's seal – the only one available to her – and stood up. She glanced at the bell-pull; she should let someone know where she was going. But she was loath to disturb the staff midday. It was one of their few times of respite.

Perhaps she could just leave a note …

"Uncle Bax!"

"Hmm?"

He nearly dropped the book he had been carrying. Her uncle had the dangerous habit of walking around the house with a book propped open, reading and walking at the same time. More than once, Daniela had seen him bump into a side table or trip over one of the plush Turkish carpets her aunt was so fond of.

Daniela grabbed his forearm to stop him from knocking over the huge blue and white Delft vase, the one she had stashed her riding clothes in, and held on until he was steady.

"Thank you, my dear. That table nearly jumped out at me."

She leaned down and picked up the book he had dropped. She offered him the thick tome. "What is so fascinating that you cannot put it down?"

"Oh, this? It's about Arabian stud lines. Your father sent it to me a few months ago."

Daniela stared at the ground. "I see."

Uncle Baxter looked awkward. His fingers drummed the cover of the book anxiously. "He has not written to you?" He finally asked.

She shook her head. "No, I'm afraid not."

"Do not take it personally, my dear. He is very busy just now. His letters may even have gone amiss in transit. Ireland is not so tame as here."

"Perhaps." Daniela nodded. It hurt too badly to say much else. Her uncle looked at her, pity in his eyes. She knew what he was thinking – for someone so young she had suffered more than her share of misfortune. Unlike his wife, who merely saw Daniela as an annoyance, he had enough heart to feel bad for her.

But she did not want nor need his pity. She straightened herself up as best she could and schooled her features to calm. "I am going into town to post a letter. I shall be back before afternoon tea."

"Yes, of course. Shall I call for the carriage?" Baxter cleared his throat and looked around for the butler, clearly grateful the awkward conversation was ending.

"No, thank you. I think I will enjoy a walk."

"Alright." Nodding, he held up his book and used it to point down the hallway. "Off I go, then."

Daniela watched him go. From the back, she could see the resemblance to her father. The Rames brothers were just a few years apart in age. She felt her heart ache for missing him. She held the letter in her hand even more tightly as she decided to eschew her pelisse and get her letter posted posthaste.

It was not a long walk into town; just under a mile once one reached the end of the long drive. Daniela wore sturdy leather boots. She'd taken to wearing them every day after her aunt had caught her coming back from the track one early afternoon with her dress on but her riding boots peeking out from underneath the hemline. To avoid suspicion, she'd started wearing boots regularly. Which her aunt thought was decidedly odd, but did not even begin to compare to how she would feel if she found out the real reason Daniela had boots beneath her dress.

In any case, her footwear was suited for the walk, the day was sunny, and although she was still worried about her father, just being outside lifted her spirits considerably.

The town was bustling with activity, mostly with young scholars slacking off on their end-of-term

One Race to Ruin

studying. The university term would end in a couple of weeks, and then the town of Cambridge would shrink considerably – the students would be headed for home, and those upper-class families who were tied to the university would set off to spend the remainder of the Season in London. But maybe she would be gone by then. It was a hopeful thought. Her plea to her father had been to bring her home as soon as possible.

Though Daniela was able to admit to herself that she would be quite disappointed to leave before the 2000 Guineas had been run.

"You there!"

"Mistress!"

"Come and have a pint with us!"

Daniela jumped at the sudden barrage of voices. They came from a knot of young men lounging in the grass adjacent to the King's Oak Tavern. University students, no doubt.

Best ignore them, she thought to herself as she continued down the road in the direction of the post office.

"Come and sit with us, ginger cat!"

She gritted her teeth. Was she going to have to start wearing her exercise-boy costume for every walk into town? Daniela continued to ignore them, crossing the street so she walked along the buildings rather than the grassy square where they were congregated.

Out of the corner of her eye she saw two of the young men stand up. One of them jogged across the street in her direction, the other loping behind.

Daniela looked around quickly, assessing her options. There was a stationary store but it looked like it was closed. Attempting to seek refuge in the King's

Oak would only exacerbate the problem; there were likely more rowdy university students within. She clenched her fists and prepared her most inhospitable expression.

The first young man reached her. His thick blond hair was long and falling forward over his brow. He had dark, mysterious eyes. In other circumstances, Daniela might have described him as dashing.

"Excuse my friends, Miss, they have no idea how to properly address a lady," he said, flashing a grin.

Daniela looked down her nose at him – as best she could given her more diminutive stature. "You ought to advise them to keep their ungentlemanly thoughts to themselves," she said without breaking step.

Instead of being put off by her crisp comment, the golden-haired young man fell into step with her.

"I'm just that sorry, Miss."

Daniela hoped that would be the end of it. But the man continued to walk with her, that irritating smile plastered to his face. His friend walked a few paces behind them. Daniela had the uncomfortable sensation of being stalked by an animal. She stubbornly refused to look at either of them directly.

"Well then, be on your way." She tried to imbue her voice with the sound of authority.

"Please, my lady, don't judge me based on that lot."

"I am not interested in company today, if you please."

"But you haven't even asked my name. How do you know you aren't interested?"

"Your name will make no difference in my disposition." Daniela reached the street where she needed to turn for the post office. However, one glance down the street revealed it empty of any other people. She was not naïve enough to walk down the street alone with two unknown and intractable young men.

She came to a halt on the corner, crossing her arms and frowning sternly. "I must insist you leave me to my business."

"I am the future Duke of Forsyth, Miss. Surely you have time for a duke," the young buck said, his chest puffing out a little. Clearly, he was used to his title eliciting a certain type of response from young women.

"Well bully for you."

His smile did not fade, but it changed to something less affable. More … malicious. Daniela couldn't help her sharp intake of breath.

Simultaneously, his lieutenant moved up behind her shoulder and the wayward future duke reached out and gripped her arm. Without thinking, Daniela grabbed his arm for leverage and rammed her knee up between his legs.

He yelped loudly, his hands immediately going around himself as he hunched over. The other young man went to his aid, pushing past her shoulder. She thought she had effectively neutralized the rude future lord but he looked up at her menacingly.

"So, the cat has claws," he sneered, his long blonde hair falling forward over his face. "Let's see about clipping them, shall we –"

"Shall you depart immediately? Yes, I think that would be the most prudent course of action."

Daniela felt the presence come up behind her, but instead of raising the hairs on the back of her neck this time she felt a wave of relief crest through her.

Eric did not need to step around her; his presence was sufficiently intimidating even standing at her shoulder. She could feel the heat of his body near to hers, the solid warm expanse extremely comforting.

"We were having a private conversation with the lady," the second young man said, his friend still working on getting back to an upright position after Daniela's well-placed blow.

Eric did not budge an inch. "I believe that I heard the young lady tell you she would prefer you departed her company."

"You misheard." Forcing himself to stand straight, the golden boy glared at Eric with impunity. "Now I demand that you leave us to our conversation, as the future Duke of Forsyth –"

"Forsyth, eh? I would have thought you would be at the University of Edinburgh, given your father's background. Perhaps I will call on him when I am next in Scotland. In the meantime, give him my regards."

"I don't –"

"Of course, you don't know who is sending their regards. The Earl of Fordham. Please tell your father I look forward to renewing our acquaintance very soon."

The future duke looked fit to burst. His companion seemed to know that they had been bested; he was tugging at his friend's shirtsleeve rather insistently.

Daniela sensed the tenseness in Eric's body as the insufferable young man stood his ground, refusing to depart. She would not let them come to fisticuffs over her. Eric had far too much to concern himself with to be dealing with the gossip surrounding a brawl with a duke's son. She turned to him, seeing his face for the first time in the exchange.

"Lord Fordham, will you do me the honor of escorting me as I finish my errands this afternoon?"

"Of course." Eric offered her his arm, which she took immediately. She nodded down the street where the post office waited. Eric obliged, turning them away from the pair of hooligans.

However, Daniela could not resist throwing one last glance over her shoulder. "Best be on your way before you embarrass yourselves further."

The young future duke's face reddened instantly with anger, while his companion's eyes flew open wide. She did not pause to see further reactions but turned and walked down the street with the Earl of Fordham at a brisk clip.

When they were a full block away, Daniela chanced a backward glance. The two young men had begun to hobble back towards their friends. She felt herself relax noticeably. Though she would most definitely have to take a more circuitous route home to avoid them.

Eric followed her gaze. "I would advise a different path when you return home."

"You've read my mind." Daniela came to a halt. "Thank you for your help. I think I could have managed them, but better not to test myself in this case."

"I saw you get your knee up. I was very impressed. And a little afraid." Eric smiled, something she had only seen him do a handful of times in their weeks-long acquaintance. Daniela felt a flush of warmth that had nothing to do with the heat of the unseasonably fair spring weather.

"I spent a lot of time in the stables growing up. My father thought it prudent that I have at least the rudiments of self-defense theory."

"Your father is a smart man in more ways than one."

The mention of her father reminded Daniela of the reason for her outing. As she reached for her pocket, she realized that their arms were still linked. "Excuse me, I —"

"Of course! I beg your pardon!" Eric released her arm immediately.

Daniela fished out the neatly folded letter. "I was on my way to the post office to see this letter sent to my father. Please, do not let me detain you."

Eric's lips curved into a wry little quirk. "I was headed there myself. I am expecting a letter from my solicitor in London and I find myself too impatient to wait for a delivery."

Daniela's heart did a fantastic little thump. "Shall we go together?"

In answer, Eric offered her his arm. She took it once again, this time completely having forgotten her altercation with the rowdy university set.

Of course, they were only a block away from the post office. There wasn't time for anything but a few awkwardly exchanged glances. Eric was quite impressed with how she had handled herself while being molested by those infernal young men. She was a fighter, that much was clear. That had been easy to see since he met her in Lord Harker's ballroom a fortnight ago.

What he did not expect were the waves of attraction that were coming hard and fast. He was ashamed to think that as a younger man, he might

One Race to Ruin

have been just as impetuous as those boys when confronted with such beauty. Her simple dove-gray dress did nothing to tamp down her attractiveness. She had forgone a cap or pelisse. The muslin fabric clung to her womanly curves as it caught the spring breeze. The brassy red of her hair was softer as they passed through a patch of shade, more of a rose gold hue.

He held open the door of the post office for her, feeling the loss of her arm in his as she stepped into the small room. A counter ran half the length of one wall. Several boxes fitted with locks, which patrons could rent individually, lined the adjacent wall. Behind the counter was a handwritten list of the cost to post letters and packages to various popular destinations: London, Newcastle, Liverpool, and so on.

Daniela stepped up to the counter. "Good afternoon. I would like to post this letter to Ireland."

Eric's ears perked up. *Ireland?*

"Of course, Miss. Whereabouts?"

"County Cork."

"Alright then, just a moment." The postal clerk stepped away to calculate the postage. Eric stepped forward, leaning against the counter. Perhaps she had misspoken earlier.

"You said you are writing to your father?" He asked.

"Yes. We've never been apart for this long," she confirmed, then turned back to the clerk. She slid the letter across the counter and then counted out the coins for the postage he recited.

"Thank you, ma'am. And how may I be of service to you, sir?" The clerk asked, turning to Eric.

"I'm expecting a letter from J.C. Burrows and Sons, in London. Directed to Eric Weathers, the Earl of Fordham."

"Ah, yes. I believe something of that nature came by special messenger this morning …" The clerk trailed off as he moved to look through the little cubicles behind him, most filled with a letter or small parcel.

Eric saw Daniela's eyebrow pop up in interest. He hoped she was too polite to ask. He'd sent a letter to his solicitor right away after that unsettling business with Bradford Kenner. He had also made a few quiet inquiries around Newmarket and Cambridge. But thus far, Eric had been unable to establish a link between his estate's financial woes and the interminably odious Kenner. And that made him feel even more disconcerted.

It seemed they both had matters they would rather not discuss.

"Here it is."

The letter was thick. Several sheets were folded together and sealed tightly. Eric resisted the urge to rip it open right there. Then he would certainly have to explain himself to Miss Rames. Instead, he tucked it into the inner breast pocket of his coat, promising himself he would open it at the first opportunity.

They thanked the postal clerk and stepped back out into the sunlit street. "Is there anywhere else I can escort you?" Eric asked. Despite his carnal desire to remain in her presence, the letter in his pocket was a weight on his chest. He was relieved when she answered.

Daniela shook her head, her red curls bouncing prettily. "I shall not take any more of your time. I am homeward bound now." She smiled ruefully. "I assure you, I shall stay out of sight of our surly new friends."

That earned a smile from Eric. He almost insisted on escorting her, at least as far as the edge of town. But he was sure she would refuse. And she had proven herself fully capable of defending herself.

"Until we meet again, Miss Rames." Eric bowed, bringing his face closer to Daniela's than ever before. Despite his desire to get on his own and rip open the letter from London, Eric felt something else flickering to life inside of him.

Then Miss Rames stepped back, a flush of pink moving up her cheeks. "Good afternoon, Lord Fordham." She bobbed a curtsey and set off quickly down the street.

Eric's heart did not slow until she disappeared around the corner opposite from where they had come minutes before. He stared after her, wondering if she had felt the same flames racing through her veins. That charming pink flush suggested she had.

But as he contemplated that another thought pushed everything else aside: the letter from his solicitor.

Eric pulled it out of his breast pocket, ripping open the seal quickly.

His Lordship the Earl of Fordham
Fordham House
Bridge Street, Cambridge

To Eric A.M.H. Weathers, the Earl of Fordham,

Our office placed inquiries into the matter you requested. While we had not yet received notification of the sale, it seems the bulk of the debts owed by your late father the Earl have recently been purchased by Mr. Bradford Kenner of Derbyshire. Enclosed are copies of the bills of sale, and the accounts which Mr. Kenner now holds.

Yours most sincerely,
John Castor Burrows, Solicitor

His mouth fell open as he reread the letter, sure his mind must be playing tricks on him. But the third time, and the fourth, the words remained unchanged. *Damn, damn, damn.*

Chapter 10

Tatum Greene was everything Dani had hoped. The first time they met, Mercury tried to take a nip of his arm. Greene answered with a swift swat on his snout. Mercury looked quite offended. The star thoroughbred had certainly never had a hand raised against him. Of course, Greene had not harmed the animal in any way, merely surprised him and asserted that he would not be fooled by the wily colt's games.

Then Greene had climbed aboard and ridden Mercury to a new personal record along the Newmarket Heath.

Dani could not help feeling a little jealous of how quickly horse and jockey took to one another. But she knew that riding on the exercise course and in an actual race were completely different things. And now that she knew just how dire things were for Eric …

how badly he needed Mercury to win this race ... she was thankful to have such a skilled jockey on board.

The 2000 Guineas was one week from tomorrow.

"How did he feel in the last quarter mile?" The trainer asked as Greene rode Mercury back to where Taylor, Eric, and Dani waited.

"Ready and willing," Greene said as he jumped down, proving himself still quite limber despite being in his late forties.

"Good. Tomorrow we'll have Dani take him out and try him at a mile and a quarter. That's longer than the 2000 Guineas, but I've got my eye on the Derby and the St. Ledger as well."

"All of them?" Dani said excitedly.

Eric's face was torn between pain and hope. "Let's get through this one first," he said.

"Aye, sir," Taylor nodded, but over Eric's shoulder he winked at the jockey and exercise rider.

Dani took Mercury's bridle in hand and started leading him back to the stable. It was a long walk – the town of Newmarket was comprised of stables, gallops of various lengths, the Jockey Club Rooms, and all of the other buildings that supported the extensive training grounds. Mercury was the last run of the day for Eric's stable. Taylor and Greene walked behind talking strategy and discussing the other entrants into the 2000 Guineas. Eric fell into step with Dani.

Her pulse quickened. Eric was relaxed – as relaxed as he ever was – walking alongside the unremarkable exercise rider. Dani felt oddly flattered. Whenever he was with her as Daniela, he was much more ... intense.

"I owe you a debt of gratitude," Eric said quietly.

One Race to Ruin 89

"What's that, my lord?"

"You were the one who suggested Greene. And you were right."

Dani stared at the ground as they walked. She was not sure what to say.

"As you heard, winning this race is extremely important for me and my family," Eric said gruffly.

Daniela couldn't help herself. "Your family, sir?"

"Yes …"

"It's only, I did not think there was anyone other than you, my lord." Daniela heard her voice going up several octaves as she spoke hastily. She cleared her throat in what she hoped was a masculine sound.

"Oh, yes, well, you are right about that. Since my father passed, I am the sole remaining member of my core family. I have a great aunt in Northumberland, and a few cousins who reside down in London," Eric explained. He still experienced the odd twinge every so often when he talked with Dani. But he also found the lad had a way of drawing him into conversation.

Eric's long strides ate up the ground quickly and Dani had to almost jog to keep up with him. But she was loath to give up any opportunity to spend time with him.

"But I hope one day to have a family of my own. Once I have rehabilitated the state of the earldom. This brings me to my point …"

Eric looked around. They had reached the stables. The buildings were teeming with people – trainers giving directions to jockeys and exercise riders, grooms walking out horses, stable boys mucking stalls and pushing wheelbarrows full of hay.

"May I have a word with you, privately?"

Dani felt her heart thump so hard in her chest it seemed to bounce off of her sternum. *You dolt, he thinks you are Dani the exercise rider!* She chastised herself. There was nothing improper about one man having a private conversation with another.

"Of course, sir," she stammered.

Eric waved down a groom, who looked at Mercury dubiously but took his rein without comment. Then Eric took Dani's shoulder – another pulse of heat and heartbeat reverberated through her – and steered her towards the back of the stable where bales of hay were stacked along the wall, under the overhang of the roof safe from the changeable English weather.

Dani looked around, her stomach roiling. They were truly alone. Most of the horses had already come in from their morning runs and thereby had already been fed or watered. There wasn't much need for anyone to come back here and fetch hay, at least for a while. The air smelled thick of horse. On one side of them the fragrant bales of hay stood taller than both of their heads. Opposite the hay was a line of tall trees, fully leafed out with their spring foliage. Dani found it oddly romantic.

Except that she was dressed as a man. Not as herself.

"Thank you for recommending Mr. Greene," Eric started.

Dani just nodded.

"Now, I must ask you one more favor. Very few people know of the state of my family's fortunes …" Eric paused uncomfortably.

She thought she knew what he was going to say next but she also knew that in a moment of gravitas

One Race to Ruin 91

such as this, an employee would keep their mouth shut and listen to their employer without interrupting.

"If you could be obliged to – keep that information to yourself, I would be even more deeply in your debt." Eric swallowed his pride, as he had done on so many occasions since assuming his title as Earl of Fordham. The luxuries of arrogant affluence which he had enjoyed as a younger man were not afforded to him now.

"Of –"

"I am willing to increase your salary, Dani, to make it worthwhile for you –"

"There is no need, my lord," Dani said firmly, unable to stop herself from interrupting him this time.

Eric's lips were pressed together into a tight, straight line.

"I will say nothing, sir. You and Taylor have been very good to me. I would not betray your confidence," Dani assured him.

She watched as the tension in Eric's face and body softened. His lips were no longer compressed into a line, but full and enticing. A man that was willing to put himself last, to sacrifice his pride to keep his family name in good standing, it spoke volumes to her – especially given her father's current predicament. He was so … handsome, honorable … *good*.

Without thinking, Dani raised herself onto her tiptoes and kissed him.

Eric jumped backward as if he had been struck by lightning.

Dani's first feeling was hurt; the next was horror.

"Please, Eric, I –"

"I, I …" Eric sputtered, his hands gripped into tight fists, his eyes wide. "I do not know what led you to believe I might be interested in such advances —" He started backing away, looking for an escape ...

"You don't understand —" Dani protested. But Eric was shaking his head.

She had no choice. She reached up and pulled off her cap, grabbing a handful of her hair and tugging it so that pins fell out like a cascade of raindrops and her bright red hair fell haphazardly down over her shoulders.

Eric thought he was having a nightmare. This could not be happening. Being kissed by his exercise rider was complication enough. But that exercise rider ... *bloody hell, it was Daniela Rames?* There would be no digging out of the scandal this would cause.

"What ..." He opened his mouth but couldn't get coherent words to come out.

This would ruin him. All of the work he had done to rebuild the estate, the gambles he had made, they would never have a chance to come to fruition if someone found out that Daniela Rames had been posing as his exercise rider. It would be all anyone would care about or listen to. His reputation, his ability to retain a trainer or staff ... all of it ruined. Eric felt his shock start to give way to something much hotter.

"What the devil are you thinking?" He said. This time his words came out steady, his voice low and gravelly.

"I am so sorry, I should not have been so forward. I ... I have never kissed someone before ..." Daniela held her cap in her hand, pulling at it nervously as she floundered on.

"Damn the kiss! Forget that nonsense!" His face was as dark as his hair. "Dressing up like a man?

One Race to Ruin

Getting yourself hired on as my exercise rider? Who is paying you? Is this some sort of sabotage? Or are you working for the creditors?" Eric demanded, advancing on her now.

Daniela swallowed hard. She fought her instincts to step back, holding her ground stubbornly. "I don't work for anyone but myself."

Eric snorted derisively. "And what interest does the Rames family have in my stable? Has your uncle bought up some of my debt too?"

"I had no idea about that until you told me," Daniela insisted.

"Until I told you," Eric repeated. "Of course, I thought I was talking to a young man, someone who could be trusted."

"And why can't a woman be trusted?"

"A woman can. You, apparently, cannot."

The warmth that Daniela had developed for Eric over the past few weeks was quickly evaporating. "Excuse me?" Her chestnut red brows were knit together, a frown on her pretty rosebud lips.

"You lied about who you were in order to get a job in my stable, and you expect me to believe you will keep my misfortune a secret when you've no incentive to?"

"I have done nothing but help you since I came on as an exercise rider! I am the reason that Mercury is running the way he is! I am the one who recommended Tatum Greene!" The hold that Daniela had kept on her tongue while working as Eric's employee was quickly coming untethered.

"You've ruined me! It's only a week until the 2000 Guineas. Mercury will not be ready, not when we have to find a new exercise rider!" Eric looked away from her, his eyes calculating, doing the math, and realizing the gravity of the predicament.

"You don't need to find a new exercise rider."

He did not respond to that for several long, hotly charged moments. The gaze that Eric brought back to her was still heated, but a little more under control.

"Are you suggesting that I keep you on? After this deception you have contrived?"

It took everything she had to keep her temper in check. Daniela took several fortifying breaths in and out through her nose, her chest heaving up and down. Eric couldn't help looking down, wondering how she had flattened those taut little breasts down ... *argh! Perish such thoughts!*

"I have not deceived you out of malice. Despite what you think," she paused, wondering how much she should tell him. Well, perhaps if she revealed something of her own misfortune he would understand her sympathy for his. "My father's name has been sullied. He has been accused of untruthfully trying to pass off a young colt as the offspring of a prize-winning stallion. Our entire farm and family name are in question."

She saw that she had Eric's attention. He crossed his arms, looking down at her with the frown still firmly fixed on his face. But his eyes were not as hard.

"My father is in Ireland trying to get to the bottom of this and restore our good name. And I am stuck here in Cambridge with my aunt and uncle."

Eric sympathized but his anger was not mollified. "You've failed to connect your troubles with your supposedly unintentional interference in mine."

Daniela nearly stamped her foot in frustration. "I wanted to reclaim some part of my identity!"

One Race to Ruin

"By hiding your identity?"

"By being around racehorses!"

"Well, your vanity has put me in an impossible spot. When this comes to light, I will be ruined. I will be the laughingstock of English racing." Eric's entire body was rigid as he spoke those words.

"Why should anyone find out? I will be careful. I've been successful so far –"

"There is no 'will' here! This charade is over," Eric insisted stubbornly.

"You've said it yourself. You don't have time to find another rider for Mercury. You have to let me stay on." Daniela knew it was a winning argument. But she also knew Eric would not accept easily. "If you let me go now your ruin is all but ensured. Mercury will fight rider after rider, lose his form, and quite possibly the race. If you keep me on, he has a real shot at winning. Not just the 2000 Guineas, but all the Classics."

"You're neglecting the risk of your identity being discovered. Your disguise is not as foolproof as you seem to think. All it took was one misguided amorous act and …"

She glared at him with such ferocity Eric trailed off mid-sentence.

"I can promise you, there will be no more *'misguided amorous acts'* on my part," Daniela said through gritted teeth.

Eric's arms were crossed so tightly against his broad chest she could see the outline of his muscles through his linen shirt and light morning coat. Just minutes ago she had been dreaming of what it would feel like to be encircled in those strong, muscular arms. *What a fool she had been!*

"You will take more care with your secret. No one must find out. Not Greene, not Taylor. No one," Eric finally said tightly.

"If Tatum has not recognized me by now, it seems unlikely he will," she said sarcastically. Eric's eyes widened again. "I will take care, I promise."

"For what that's worth."

She had had enough of his barbs. "If you will excuse me, *my lord*, I ought to see that your prize horse is settled." She leaned over and collected a handful of pins that had fallen to the ground. Mindless of the fact that they had been laying in the dirt, she shoved them into her hair and pulled her cap back into place. She walked determinedly past Eric without looking at him. "See that you don't kiss anyone on your way out."

Chapter 11

Daniela rode for Cambridge like she was trying to win the 2000 Guineas herself. Her righteous anger kept her fueled, urging her mount on even as her legs started to cramp and her hands ached from holding the reins so tightly.

He was mad at her? She had saved him! She was the only reason his precious horse even had a chance at the Classics!

The deep-abiding sympathy she had felt for him, the connection — both of their cherished homes and ways of life in such peril — it had been so endearing, helping her see past the earl's surly exterior to his warm heart beneath. But now ... *oh, she just wanted to stomp on his foot and curse.*

She was so deep in her thoughts she rode right past the little grove of trees where she usually stopped to change out of her riding clothes and back into her gown. She rode right up to the front gates of her uncle's house and then turned her horse to circle around the back, as had become her habit. Daniela stopped the horse just before the turn to come into view of the stable. She shifted her weight to one booted foot and swung her leg over the saddle to dismount, thinking to herself how much easier it was in breeches –

She was still wearing breeches!

Her first reaction was to jump back against the brick wall that edged the courtyard and house, as if plastering her back to the red stones would somehow make her disappear from view were someone to round the corner.

She couldn't go back, Daniela realized. The horse she'd been riding was tired from the grueling pace she had set riding home. Her clothes were in a shoulder bag, hanging from a branch in the secluded little stand of trees that she'd been using as a dressing room. By the time she walked back, changed her clothes, and returned, it would be well past afternoon tea time and her aunt would be looking for her.

"*¡Estúpida! ¡Estúpida! ¡Estúpida!*" She chided herself, knocking her head back against the brick wall in frustration.

Another thought entered her mind as if knocked loose by her repetitive motion. The longer she stood here, the greater her chances of being discovered.

Taking a deep breath for courage, she inched along the brick wall. Her horse was grazing on grass nonchalantly, probably just glad he was not being ridden anymore. Daniela reached the corner. She listened carefully, trying to determine who was in the stable yard beyond.

One Race to Ruin

She did not hear any voices, no conversations happening. But she did hear the repetitive sound of a broom, and every few seconds the nicker or foot-stamp of horses. *Gracias a Dios*, the yard was not busy.

Dani peeked around the corner of the wall very slowly. Her ears had heard right: there was a stable hand sweeping the dirt from the aisle out into the courtyard and two horses in the small paddock that adjoined the front of the eight-stall stable. She alternated which horse she took from her uncle's small string so she wasn't always tiring out the same one.

Despite her horrendous luck so far, the stable hand was not one she recognized.

Alright, I can do this. A plan was forming in her head. She could brazen it out. She would just have to be quick and efficient so that no one else had time to come into the stable yard.

She grabbed the horse's rein and strode boldly around the corner. The stable hand looked up, a confused look on his face. He recognized the horse but not the person accompanying him. *Good.*

"Ho there," she said, stepping right back into the persona of Dani the exercise rider. "Mistress Rames left this old boy in town. She had another errand to attend to. Gave me a shilling to bring him back for her."

The stable boy still looked confused. "Why didn't she just wait and ride him back herself?"

"Is it your place to question a lady?" Dani said, trying to make her voice sound incredulous.

The young man looked duly chastened. "Of course not, I —"

"Of course not! I was paid to deliver the steed, not to make small talk. Here!" Dani shoved the reins into the boy's hand and then turned and walked away as quickly as she could manage without arousing suspicion. Or at least she hoped.

She sagged against the brick wall with relief. That was the first hurdle managed.

But she still had to get back inside the house and up to her rooms without being detected. Sighing, she gritted her teeth.

By some miracle, Dani made it through the garden door, down the servants' hall, into the foyer, and up the stairs without meeting anyone. Her luck must finally be turning. And about time, after a day like this. All she wanted was to rip these blasted boy's clothes off, unbind her breasts, and sink into a hot bath.

As she reached the landing of the next floor and found the hallway deserted, she knew she was safe. Dani nearly skipped down the hallway to her bedroom door.

She threw open the door, already unbuttoning her vest, and nearly tripped over her cousin.

"Winnie!"

"Sir! You cannot be in here!" Winnie shrieked.

"You don't understand, I –"

"Get out!" Winnie was apparently a quicker thinker than Dani had ever given her credit for. The buxom blonde young woman took two steps and grabbed the fire poker with the ease of an experienced fencer.

"Winnie, no, it's me!" Daniela ripped the cap from her head for the second time today, not even feeling the tug of the pins in her hair as they were torn out of place – more than a few of her long red locks going with them.

Winnie dropped the poker with a loud clang that had both young women wincing. *Por favor, no dejes que la tía Millie lo escuche,* Daniela prayed silently.

"Daniela – what are you wearing?" Winnie took several steps backward, her eyes wide with shock.

"I, Winnie, please …" Daniela's eyes flew towards the door. She needed to get there before her cousin, close the damn thing, and plant herself in front of it until she could convince her cousin –

"I won't tell anyone."

"What?" Daniela froze, turning around slowly to look at her cousin.

"I won't tell anyone your secret," Winnie said again, looking queerly at Daniela.

"I … I don't know what to say … I thought that –"

"That I would want to tell my mother?" Winnie finished for her.

"Well, yes." Daniela flushed, but could not deny the truth of the words.

"I do think that she would be terribly mad," Winnie said, coming to sit beside Daniela on the upholstered bench. "But I don't think she needs to know everything. And I don't think she needs to know about … this. Whatever it is …" A little giggle escaped as she motioned towards her cousin's attire.

Daniela glanced down at her rumpled shirt, dirty breeches, and unbuttoned vest hanging loose around her shoulders. She burst into giggles as well. Once she started laughing she could not stop. All of the tension and fears of the last several hours bubbled over into uncontrollable laughter.

Instead of looking at her as if she were insane – which would have been entirely justifiable – Winnie joined in Daniela's contagious laughter.

The two young women laughed together on the little upholstered bench until their sides ached and each breath came as a desperate gasp.

Finally, they started to catch their breaths. The heave of their chests slowed. There was silence between them, but perhaps for the first time it was laced with camaraderie rather than awkwardness.

"May I ask … what *is* all of this about?" Winnie touched the frayed edge of Daniela's shirtsleeve tentatively.

Daniela sighed. "*This* is a very long story."

Winnie raised her eyebrows eagerly.

When Daniela sighed again, this time a little chuckle escaped as well.

"Help me get cleaned up and changed, and I will start at the beginning."

Chapter 12

Eric could not believe his misfortune. It seemed like a cruel joke was being practiced upon him – first Bradford Kenner buying up his debt and then Daniela Rames posing as his exercise rider? What nonsense would the universe come up with next?

He arrived at Lady Laurel St. Marten's annual party with deep resentment and frustration in his gut. He'd attended with his father every year since he was sixteen years old. Lady St. Marten had been holding her annual soiree on the Friday two weeks prior to the 2000 Guineas for as long as most people in the Newmarket racing scene could remember.

She invited all of the owners with entrants in the race, whether they were usual members of *ton* society or not. Many members of society traveled from London just to attend the storied event. If it had been anyone other than Lady St. Marten, or any other event, Eric would have begged off and stayed home to grouchily drink brandy in his study.

But people would notice if he did not attend. He was the Earl of Fordham. He'd entered a horse in the 2000 Guineas for the first time in a decade. And rumors were flying about the solvency of his family estate. No, he had to attend. Bugger it.

He dressed to suit his mood: black breeches, a midnight blue waistcoat, and a black tailcoat. His dark hair capped off the imposing outfit. The only patch of brightness was the stark white cravat tied expertly at his throat.

His butler tried to bring around the carriage but Eric eschewed it in favor of Cerberus. He ignored his man's pained look as he climbed aboard his horse. Eric did not care if he turned up to the party rumpled. They were lucky he was turning up at all.

Tomorrow morning, he would have to return to Newmarket and face Daniela Rames – he would have to watch her ride out on his prized racehorse, his last best hope for saving his family fortune – and act as if everything were perfectly normal.

As if she had not put his entire future in jeopardy with her charade. As if those tight men's breeches did not hug every curve of her perfect derriere …

He shook his head forcefully. That was *not* a line of thought that could be allowed. He'd been attracted to Daniela when he met her at the track and later in the village. He'd been willing to revise his impression of her once. But a fourth meeting was all it took to convince him he'd judged her correctly the first time they danced at Lord Harker's ball. Something about

Dani had been amiss since the beginning and now Eric knew what it was.

As he steered his horse out of the courtyard and onto the road, he pulled the pocket watch from his breast pocket and flipped the engraved gold cover open. It was going on ten o'clock in the evening. He would stay at this blasted event for exactly one hour. Then he would come home and maybe find some peace in sleep. For it certainly could not be found anywhere else in his ridiculous life.

Daniela almost stayed home. Not because she wanted to, but because she had words with her aunt over her choice of gown.

She wore a bright crimson-red silk gown. The fitted sleeves ended just above her elbows and the neckline was a large square that scooped low over her breasts. Beneath her bust were several craftily placed darts, nipping the silk in so that her trim waist was well-defined.

"You look like a harlot."

"This dress is no different than the one I wore the other evening!" Daniela protested.

"That is absurd. The color is completely inappropriate for a respectable woman, let alone an unmarried debutante!" Aunt Millie's cheeks had colored brightly enough they almost matched the color of Daniela's gown.

Daniela forced herself to take a deep breath. *She wasn't a debutante*, she wanted to remind her aunt.

Unlike Winnie, there had been no presentation at court, no debutante ball, and no prospective suitors. And that was exactly how Daniela wanted it!

But her aunt wasn't done. She turned to her husband.

"This is what happens when a girl doesn't have a mother. She's had no one to teach her proper decorum!"

The color drained out of Daniela's face. She was not easily given to tears, but she felt an unfamiliar stinging in the corners of her eyes. She turned back towards the stairs with every intent of slamming her bedroom door and never speaking to her aunt again.

But her uncle intervened. "That's enough, Millie. Let's go."

"Husband, you can't –"

"The child has suffered enough," *without you adding to it*, was the unspoken subtext that entered the room as potently as if he had said the words aloud.

Millie looked surprised to be chastened by her husband. She shot a contemptuous glance at her niece, who was still frozen at the foot of the stairs. Then she grabbed Winnie's arm and stomped out the door to the waiting carriage.

Daniela opened her mouth to say something to her uncle but he shook his head. Unable to meet her eyes, he followed his wife and daughter outside.

She stood for several seconds more, her hand on the railing. She determined she would not speak to her aunt for the rest of the night. Longer if she could manage it.

"Would you like to dance? I can introduce you to some gentlemen that I know …"

Daniela felt a little candle of warmth flicker inside of her. Since they had arrived, Winnie had been making kind offers and suggestions. As Winnie had helped her rinse her hair and brush out the long red curls, she had listened to her cousin's story with an open-heartedness that was completely unexpected. She had misjudged her, thinking her a miniature of her aunt. Winnie was painfully awkward at times, but beneath that veneer was a sweetheart.

"Thank you, but I'd rather not. I'm not in the mood for it tonight." Daniela squeezed Winnie's hand affectionately. Winnie smiled, her rounded cheeks curving prettily against her bouncing blonde curls.

"Will you be alright? I don't want to leave you alone. Oh, hello Mr. Rayden!" Winnie jumped when a young man joined them.

"Miss Rames," the young man bowed first to Winnie and then Daniela.

"I thought your family had gone to London." Winnie squeezed Daniela's hand. Curious, Daniela glanced between her cousin and the young man. Winnie was blushing a delicate and very becoming shade of pink.

It was the same young man from Lord Harker's ball, Daniela realized. She'd thought him quite nice looking then. When he looked at Winnie his smile lit his entire face. With his slightly rounded build, he looked like an affable, friendly bear. No wonder Winnie was beaming.

"My father's horse is entered in the 2000 Guineas," Mr. Rayden explained.

"Of course," Winnie trailed off awkwardly. She glanced around, casting about for something else to say. "This is my cousin! Daniela Rames! She loves horses!"

Daniela cringed for Winnie. Small talk with her was liable to drive even the most persistent suitor away. But Mr. Rayden was still here; that was interesting.

"Don't we all?" Mr. Rayden joked. Winnie giggled. Daniela tried not to roll her eyes. "I'm pleased to meet you, Miss Rames. You must meet the gentleman I was just speaking to. He has a horse entered in the race as well!"

Mr. Rayden turned to motion someone else forward. Through the parting crowd, Daniela saw the shining black hair. Now it was she who was squeezing Winnie's hand to the point of pain.

"Miss Daniela and Miss Winnie, this is Eric Weathers, the Earl of Fordham. We have only just met this evening, but his horse Mercury is running in the 2000 Guineas as well."

Their gazes met, her darker eyes finding his blue ones, as clear and pale as the morning sky. Daniela could feel her pulse beating wildly: in her wrist, her throat, her chest – all pounding in intense unison.

Winnie squeezed her hand back. She looked wildly from Daniela to Eric and back again. She opened her mouth. "I ... I see," she floundered, failing miserably to say anything to take the edge off of the moment.

Luckily, Mr. Rayden was far too focused on Winnie herself to notice the byplay between Daniela and Eric.

"Miss Rames, would you do the honor of dancing with me?" His eyes were on Winnie, his adoring look now completely ignored by a preoccupied Daniela.

But his words did get her attention. Her eyes flew to Winnie, who looked horribly torn between accepting the suit of a young man she was clearly interested in and not leaving her cousin alone with the very object of her discomfiture.

Daniela forced her face to neutrality. "Go on, Winnie. Do enjoy yourself." She released Winnie's hand, inclining her head toward Mr. Rayden and trying to give her cousin an encouraging smile. Winnie looked less than convinced, but she accepted Mr. Rayden's outstretched hand and followed him onto the dance floor.

Eric stood still as a stone beside Daniela as they watched the other couple depart.

"What are you doing here?" He hissed.

She shot him an irritated look. "I was invited."

"Your uncle was invited."

"The effect is the same," she said testily. "No one is forcing you to stand here and talk to me."

"We were introduced, specifically. It would be rude of me to depart so *abruptly*." He emphasized the last word, hoping she would recognize the subtle dig about their first social meeting at Lord Harker's ball weeks before.

"I'm shocked to find such a thing matters to someone who is *so* habitually rude –"

"*I* am rude? You are the most—"

"Yes?" Daniela challenged, her pert little nose high in the air.

Eric glared down at her through narrowed eyes. "I think we have conversed long enough to satisfy our onlookers."

"And here I thought you were about to ask me to dance," she said, her eyes wide with mock innocence.

"I have suffered enough discomfort at your hands for one day, Miss Rames."

Daniela's face flushed angrily, the redness climbing her cheeks and reaching her hairline in seconds.

"How dare you," she breathed.

"Fordham!"

Eric felt like someone had dumped ice down the back of his shirt.

Daniela turned to meet the new arrival, trying to push down her anger and praying her blush had faded even fractionally.

The man who joined them grabbed Eric's hand familiarly, but the look on Eric's face was acutely pained.

"Glad to see you here, old friend. I was afraid you might not have the … well, I was afraid we might not see you tonight." The smile on his face was dark. An instant distaste started to take root inside Daniela, just as the man turned his eyes on her. "Who is your lovely companion?"

If Eric had been upset by the casual way that Kenner was speaking to and handling him, his blood started to boil when he saw the way the man looked at Daniela. He raked his eyes over her appreciatively, his gaze lingering unapologetically on her amply showcased breasts.

One Race to Ruin 111

Instinctively, Eric moved closer to her. "Miss Daniela Rames, this is Mr. Bradford Kenner, an *acquaintance* from the racing circuit."

The air was thickly charged. Daniela was intensely aware of Eric, his arm just an inch away from touching hers. She also caught the malignant cloud that passed over Kenner's face, though he hid it very quickly and effectively.

"Good evening, Mr. Kenner." Daniela technically curtsied, but it was the barest gesture of respect. She did not know what was between this man and Eric, but despite their differences, she certainly knew whose side she would be on.

"Give me credit where it's due, Fordham! An opponent! My horse will be running against yours in the 2000 Guineas." Kenner leaned towards Daniela, winking lasciviously. "Place your bets on me, missy, if you want to win."

"Is your wife with you tonight?" Eric interjected. Kenner ignored him.

"I've seen Lord Fordham's horse run. I know where I will be placing my bets," Daniela said coolly. Eric felt a surge of something in his chest that he didn't care to identify.

Kenner rocked back on his heels. One pudgy hand came up to stroke his stubbly chin. "You like a long shot."

"I like to win." Daniela countered.

While Eric was thoroughly enjoying watching Daniela take the infuriating man to task, he also had no faith in her ability to control her wilder impulses. Without asking, he reached out, took her hand, and placed it in the crook of his arm.

"I'm afraid I must break this off. Miss Rames and I were just about to go take the air. Excuse us, Kenner." He steered Daniela away from Kenner, using his solid build and strong grip to hold her at his side while he navigated her through the crowd. She did not protest as they stepped outside.

"That man is the most odious, vexing, smarmy –"

"You have no idea." Eric's pace slowed, but he continued along the long, narrow terrace that ran the length of Lady St. Marten's mansion.

It was a cool night. Though the doors were thrown open to let in some fresh air to the crush of people inside, once outside the temperature dropped considerably. Daniela felt herself leaning in closer to Eric out of an instinctual desire to share his warmth.

"How do you know him?" Daniela asked.

Eric wanted to answer her fully and explain just how deep the tensions ran between him and Kenner. But this was not the time. "It is complicated."

"Does it have to do with your father's estate?" She asked.

A chill went through him and he remembered that he was supposed to be angry with her. Yes, the intensity of his disaffection for Kenner had everything to do with his father's estate. *His estate*, now. Just like his frustration with her ruse was entirely due to the danger it presented to his goals. His hopes.

He was about to extricate his arm from hers when he saw a shiver shake her delicate shoulders. "We should go back inside."

Daniela shook her head. The two red curls that she had left dangling beside her left ear swung tantalizingly against her neck. "Not yet."

"Then here," Eric took back his arm and shrugged off his tailcoat as Daniela watched in surprise. "Take this for now," he said as he stepped behind and draped it over her.

Daniela breathed in sharply as Eric's hands touched her shoulders, even through the thickness of his double-layered coat. She knew intuitively that his hands would be strong from years spent working with horses. He was not the type of owner who watched from a distance. But having those strong hands grip her shoulders even for just a moment sent a jolt of desire through her.

Behind her, Eric watched as her chest rose and fell with her breath. Her breasts swelled upwards within the neckline of her ferociously red gown. The delicate line of her jaw quivered so slightly he would not have noticed if he had not been standing right behind her. Without accounting for his actions, he leaned down and touched his lips to the soft spot behind her ear that her curls had brushed moments before.

Daniela gasped. Her eyes fluttered closed as intense heat spread from the spot where his lips touched her skin all through her body.

Once he started Eric could not stop himself. His hands still on her shoulders, he turned her slowly around to face him. He looked down into her eyes for one moment, searching for the fire of anger or a demand to stop. But all he saw was eagerness and desire that matched his own. He lowered his lips to hers, letting the spark of longing that had been lit that afternoon behind the stable at Newmarket take control.

She welcomed him in. Her mouth opened to his instantly. Daniela had never kissed a man before but her body seemed to know what to do and she listened. When his tongue slid against hers at the same time that his hand slid beneath the coat and along her spine, her mouth and hips answered back, arching against him. It was the most intoxicating feeling, like riding headlong in the wind, but more ...

A loud explosion of applause spilled onto the terrace from inside. Both of them turned instinctively towards the sound, their mouths parting. Eric felt a profound and immediate sense of loss that would disturb him when he reflected on it later. Daniela was a-jumble with emotions and sensations she barely understood.

When no one emerged immediately onto the terrace to join them, they turned back to each other. Eric released Daniela, stepping back to put a few inches of cool air between them.

"I am sorry for putting your hopes in jeopardy. That was never my intent," Daniela said softly.

Eric frowned. It was much easier to be mad at her when she was defiant and prideful. When she wasn't standing in his tailcoat, her lips sexily swollen from his kiss.

"No one can find out," he finally said.

Daniela nodded her head emphatically. "Mercury must win," she said, though a part of her wondered if he meant that no one must find out about her identity ... or about the interlude they had just shared.

"Alright."

"I think we ought to return inside. Winnie will be looking for me."

"Of course." Eric offered her his arm, which she reached to accept, only then realizing that she still wore his tailcoat. She laughed and he chuckled. A sound Daniela had heard so rarely from him it made her heart stop.

Reluctantly, she let him lift the jacket from her shoulders and watched as he pulled it back on. She was sorry to see his broad chest, much more visible in just his shirt, disappear beneath the stiffer fabric.

He escorted her back inside. Both of them were acutely aware of the other's closeness, and of the increasing folds of complexity that were layering onto them faster than either could keep up with.

Chapter 13

Taylor decided to rest Mercury on Saturday and Sunday, so it was not until Monday morning when she showed up at Newmarket that Dani saw Eric again.

Just like she had a dozen times before, she rode into the training grounds, tied up her horse in a paddock, and walked the few hundred yards to where the Earl of Fordham's string of racehorses was stabled. But unlike every other time, her eyes were sharp and her heart was pounding. She could hear the blood rushing in her ears.

Dani did not know whether she was hoping to see him or not to see him. It was a moot point, she reminded herself. He had never missed a training session.

She entered the stable, walking down the long aisle to Mercury's stall. A groom was inside the stall

One Race to Ruin

already saddling him. The churlish colt was pawing the ground with his hoof.

"Hold yer temper, ye great beast," the groom scolded, tightening down the girth.

Mercury saw her and gave his stately head a great shake. "Ye damn snake!" The groom cried, trying to catch the reins as the horse jolted forward. Dani caught the bridle in her hand and held it firmly.

"Behave, young man," she said sternly, patting his cheek firmly. Mercury rewarded her by mouthing at her vest pockets looking for treats. "None for you 'til we've had our run." She pushed his snout away.

"You've the courage of God himself, gettin' aboard this beast." The groom shook his head, giving the saddle a final tug to make sure it was firmly cinched in place.

"He's not so bad," Dani said affectionately. She reached up to tweak Mercury's forelock, his shiny mane almost the same shade as her own glossy curls, pinned up beneath her cap.

The groom watched the interplay between horse and rider with a look of amazement on his face. "If I tried that, he'd 've nipped me fingers clean off."

Dani decided not to advise the poor young man that his jumpiness did nothing but rile up the naturally high-strung horse. "I'll take him up to the training gallop," she said instead.

"Suit yourself, man." The groom backed off, a grateful look on his face.

"*Vamos, mi gran monstruo,*" Dani crooned as she led Mercury out into the aisle, kicking the stall door closed behind her.

"Your mother is Spanish."

Dani nearly jumped out of her skin.

Eric reached instinctively for Mercury's rein, but even in her surprise Dani managed to keep ahold of it. Their hands brushed; he yanked his back quickly as if burned.

Dani cleared her throat. "Yes, as I said when we first met."

"When I first met Dani."

"I am Dani."

"Do people really call you that?" Eric quirked an eyebrow curiously. He was leaning casually against the stall door that abutted Mercury's. The stall was unoccupied; Mercury had a reputation not just for nipping human flesh, but horseflesh as well.

Dani nodded. "My father does, and my mother did."

"Did?"

"She died when I was very young."

"Is she the one who taught you to ride … the way you do?"

A smile grew on Dani's face. Eric had not said it explicitly but his admiration for her riding skill had been clear in his tone. "I was hardly walking when she died. But my father was determined that I should know my Spanish heritage. He hired Spanish language tutors, learned to speak it himself, and practiced with me. He paid a fortune to bring Spanish riding instructors to the farm so I would learn to ride in the Spanish style."

"Did your father see action, in Spain?"

"Yes – at the Siege of San Sebastian. That is where he met my mother."

Eric nodded. Many English soldiers had taken foreign lovers during the wars with Napoleon. Not many had married them and brought them back to

English shores. Her mother must really have been someone special.

Mercury stomped his hoof impatiently, giving an irritated little whinny. He'd been saddled and he knew what that meant. He was itching to run.

Eric tilted his head down the aisle. "Let's go."

Dani followed him out. Eric was appalled at himself. Until the damn horse had started making a nuisance of himself, he'd been ready to pull Dani into the empty stall and take up where they had left off three nights before.

He thought she'd looked appealing in that luscious red gown with the swell of her breasts spilling over the neckline and her lips quivering with anticipation. That was nothing to how she looked now. Her breasts might be bound – he was sure they were – none of their ripe curves were discernable beneath shirt and vest. But the breeches she wore fit her hips and backside snuggly, displaying womanly curves that he could not believe he had failed to notice in all their prior training sessions.

He forced himself to walk in front of her down the aisle and out of the stable. Just so he would not be tempted to stare.

Taylor saved him from any further improper thoughts by appearing a few yards outside of the stable yard to walk with them up to the training gallop.

"I met with Greene yesterday," Taylor began. Then he saw Dani a few paces behind and stopped until the exercise rider caught up. "You'd best hear this too, lad."

Eric and Dani exchanged looks but neither said anything.

Taylor noticed nothing strange, plowing on with his explanation. "I met with Greene yesterday. I've been watching the other horses entered in the field, talkin' with Greene about who's up to ride each of 'em. There's not a lot of speed in the race, that's to our advantage I think. Mercury can take it slow and save the burst of energy for the end when the closers make their move."

Dani's eyebrows shot up. "He's going to hate that."

"Probably," Taylor agreed. "He likes to have his way. So, Greene will keep him near the front but hold him in check until the last quarter mile or so. Then give him full reign."

"It sounds reasonable," Eric agreed. "What about Midnight Destiny? I looked at his times. They are close to Mercury's."

"Kenner's horse?" Taylor shook his head dismissively. "They've only been running him on flat gallops. The Rowley Mile undulates. If he's to make good on those times he'll have to pick it up."

Eric was tempted to argue but he shoved his worry down. Taylor had not led him astray yet.

Taylor turned back to Dani. "When you take him out today, lad, I want you to keep him tight for the first three-quarters. He will fight you, I'm sure of it. But let's get him accustomed to saving it for the end."

Philosophically, Dani thought it was a decent plan. As the one who would be atop Mercury during this trial run, she was less than convinced. A more willful horse she'd never met.

They reached the training course a few minutes later. Without thinking about it, Eric turned to offer the exercise rider a leg up. He had been thinking so deeply about the training plan, it wasn't until his left hand was cradling her knee that he remembered just *who* he was helping into the saddle.

He felt Dani tense in his hands. But there was no going back now. He slid his right hand down her shin to her ankle. Eric thought he heard her gasp but he could not be sure. And then he had launched her upwards. She landed gracefully, perfectly astride, her toned thighs gripping Mercury's sides.

Eric swallowed hard.

Dani's hands gripped the reins so hard her knuckles practically glowed white.

A touch that had a week before been completely casual and nonchalant had shaken both of them deeply.

Eric cleared his throat. "Have a good ride," he said gruffly. He turned to join Taylor and head for the finish, where they would be able to better watch the entire run.

Dani watched him go, her eyes glued to his broad shoulders, rising and falling as he strode away. She closed her eyes and tried to force herself to focus. Lord knew that if she did not, Mercury would punish her for it.

When she opened her eyes a minute later she felt a bit steadier. She nudged Mercury forward, hoping that by the time she put him through his warm-ups she would have all of her faculties about her again.

Eric watched from afar as she trotted and then cantered Mercury in wide loops. She sat the horse so gracefully; as if they were one. It was quite shocking, considering how she stomped around the dance floor. He swallowed down the fire burning in his throat and turned his feet towards the finish line.

Out of the corner of his eye, he saw Bradford Kenner leaning against the rail near the entrance to the training gallop. Eric could feel the beady, calculating eyes following him as he walked, but he did not stop or glance in the other man's direction.

A few minutes later he came to stand beside Taylor. The trainer's pipe hung from the corner of his mouth, his stopwatch in his hand. The flag dropped at the other end of the practice course and the run was off. Eric stared down the course, his mind silently ticking the seconds. He was surprised when one minute ticked by, then a minute fifteen. Mercury and Daniela were just passing the three-quarter-mile pole. Then something switched on; horse and rider thundered across the finish line.

Taylor clapped him hard on the back. "Dani's done it."

Dani was grinning from ear-to-ear as she brought Mercury back around at a trot. "How fast was the last quarter?" She asked breathlessly.

"Twenty-two seconds," Taylor said, his grizzled face curving into a slightly lopsided smile.

Eric wanted to pull her off of the horse and kiss the smile right off of her face. He wanted those full, rose-pink lips on his, the hands that deftly held the reins on his shoulders as they had been last night.

Instead, he cleared his throat, clenched and unclenched his fists at his sides, and tried to get ahold of himself.

Taylor grabbed Mercury's reins and offered a hand up to Dani to help her down.

"He fought me the whole first quarter, pulling *hard*," Dani recounted as her feet hit the ground. The trio – or foursome, horseflesh included – started

One Race to Ruin

walking slowly back towards the start of the course. "By the time we hit the half-mile he had settled in. But when I asked him to run …" A look of dreamy satisfaction came over her face; Eric wondered if she would look the same spread out on a bed.

"We'll have Tatum take him out tomorrow," Taylor said, already calculating. The race is Saturday. We'll do a light workout on Thursday, and nothing at all on Friday. I want him raring and ready when he steps onto the Rowley Mile."

Dani nodded along in agreement. "So, I'll take him out Wednesday and Thursday?"

"Yes. But I want both you and Greene here every morning until the race. I don't want to disrupt this temperamental beast's routine." This time the admonition was accompanied by a friendly pat on the chestnut rump.

Taylor turned to Eric to discuss another horse from the Earl of Fordham's stable that would be up next. Dani took the opportunity to slyly observe Eric. He was always so tense at the beginning of a run; it was like every time he saw her and Mercury's success, he was reassured and able to relax a bit. She liked that she was able to give that to him – a little bit of solace and comfort. The high-strung man needed it.

She had never ridden a horse quite like Mercury. He was special. And riding him was an honor. She would have to thank Eric, at some point, for letting her. Eric might doubt, but Dani was completely certain that Mercury was destined for greatness.

They neared the entrance of the training gallop. Eric and Taylor were still deep in conversation, seeming to have forgotten about the exercise rider who walked along with them. Mercury certainly hadn't forgotten, however. He must have thought he wasn't getting the attention a magnificent racehorse like he was due, for he reached over and nibbled at Dani's ear.

She laughed and swatted his snout away, but not before he upset her cap. Dani grabbed for it instinctively but it was already loosened by the intensity of their ride. She caught it before it hit the ground but not before her head of carefully pinned red hair was revealed.

It was back on in an instant. Mere seconds passed. Dani held it in place, her heart pounding rapidly. She was afraid to look around her. One hand on her head, the other clenched at her side, she forced herself to look up.

By some miracle, as her eyes scanned behind and beside the small group, no one seemed to be staring or acting unusually. The Newmarket training grounds were intensely busy during the spring meeting, it was true, but everyone here had business they were about, she reminded herself. No one was paying attention to a lowly exercise rider.

Then she caught sight of the pudgy, greasy-haired man from three nights before. She froze in place.

Mercury kept walking, Taylor at his lead, but Eric noticed something was amiss. He took two long steps back to stand beside Dani.

"What is it?"

"I … Mercury nipped at me, and my cap fell off. Just for a moment …"

"Devil creature," Eric cursed, shaking his head. "Did anyone see …" He followed Dani's gaze.

Bradford Kenner was leaning back against the rail with an oily smile on his face.

"No," Eric breathed, unable to believe their misfortune.

"He can't have seen." Dani shook her head, reassuring herself. "It was just a moment, two or three seconds. My hair was still pinned up. And he's at a distance. He's only met me once. How would he possibly recognize me?"

"Your hair is very distinctive, Daniela." It was the first time Eric had used her full name. She wished she could have heard it from his lips in any other situation or moment.

"He can't know," she protested weakly. Kenner watched them for another moment with that terrible smile on his face. Then he turned back to the rail to watch the next horse starting to gallop. "See? He certainly would have said something!"

"I am not so sure." Eric stared hard at the other man's back. Kenner loved to gloat, as he'd proven since taking control of the bulk of Eric's father's debts. If he wasn't doing so now, maybe it stood to reason … but the man could also be devious. There was no doubt in Eric's mind about that.

"We have to be more careful," Eric said with a grim sigh.

Dani nodded circumspectly, feeling guilty even though she knew she had done nothing wrong.

"Let's go."

Chapter 14

When the day's training runs finished, Eric did not go back to the Jockey Club Rooms as he usually would. He might have enjoyed a cup of brandy-fortified tea and perhaps some conversation with one of the many acquaintances who would be flooding in all week from London. It might have taken his mind off of his financial worries – and off of the curve of Dani's legs in those breeches, which seemed to be burned into his consciousness.

But he did not want to risk running into Kenner again. He did not want the opportunity for his worst fears to be confirmed. What would happen if Dani's identity were revealed? Eric did not think there were any explicit rules about a woman exercise rider – though now that he thought of it, it might be time to consult the Jockey Club's formal charter and rules.

One Race to Ruin

No, the real risk was scandal. Ruin. Shame. He had but one chance to pull his family fortunes back from the brink of disaster. A scandal of that magnitude would make it impossible to retain staff and upset Mercury's chances not only at the 2000 Guineas but the other Classics. And the rest of the horses in his string, who were just beginning to turn a profit? They would all be rider-less, trainer-less, hopeless.

So instead of the Jockey Club Rooms, he headed for a pub. Not a normal place to find a young earl. Just the type of place frequented by the wolfish university scoundrels who had tried to take advantage of Daniela the other week. But the perfect place to have a pint of ale undisturbed, in a darkened corner.

"Afternoon! What'll ye have, sir?" The portly barkeep yelled when Eric entered the shadowy pub. There were a few oil lamps on the bar, none on the tables. The only light came from the afternoon sun spilling in through the thick, cloudy glass windows.

"Ale." Eric nodded towards a table against the far wall.

"As you'll have it, sir." The barkeep pulled out a tankard and Eric ensconced himself against the wall. He propped one booted foot on his opposite knee and leaned back. At this time of day, there was only one other patron: a middle-aged man who looked well into his cups considering it was only three o'clock in the afternoon.

The barkeep brought the ale. Eric took a sip, then leaned back his head against the scarred wooden paneling of the wall. He finally allowed himself to relax.

For the first time, his thoughts did not go to the account books or the training regimen Taylor had set up. The chestnut on his mind was of a completely different sort.

It was not that Eric was unfamiliar with women. He'd met, and consorted with, his fair share when he first went to London in his late teens. But now, at twenty-seven and with the responsibility of his family's estate firmly on his shoulders, it was different. It had to be. As a young buck, he had the security of a future earldom and the riches associated with it to back up any mistakes he might make.

Now? He had little to offer a woman but gruffness and strife. Daniela had managed to break through one, but the other was insurmountable.

He took another long draw of ale, enjoying the bitterness of it. He closed his eyes, just for a moment. Images of her in that ravishing red gown came to his mind, as he had known they would. The gown had obscured the shapely, muscled curves of her legs. He had seen those today, touched her while he gave her a leg up into the saddle. Her exercise rider costume covered her plump breasts, but last night they had been on full display. It was like putting together the most delightful puzzle in his mind ...

Eric's fantasy was broken by the scrape of chairs. Two, being pulled out directly across from him. Two men sat down – one dressed in a brown tweed suit, wearing a very severely cut mustache. Neat, not friendly. The other was huge.

The Earl of Fordham considered himself a big man. He knew his broad chest and arms, built from years of working directly with his father's horses, made him an imposing figure. But the bruiser who sat across from him now looked like he could pick up and toss Eric without a drip of sweat marring his brow.

"Gentleman, I do not believe we are acquainted," Eric said slowly, though he had a definite sense of what this was about.

"You are the Earl of Fordham," the neatly dressed tweed-man said promptly.

"Indeed. And you are …?"

"Agents of interested parties."

"That's ominous."

"Do you think so? Word was that you were feeling quite confident in your entry into the 2000 Guineas."

Eric opened his mouth to speak, but the barkeep appeared. "Ale for ye, sirs?"

"Wine, not watered." The tweed-man flicked his thumb towards his companion. "Whiskey for my associate. It helps him …" he turned his eyes back to Eric, "stay loose."

Eric took a drink of his ale, letting the bitterness anchor him.

"As I said, we are very interested in the outcome of the race Saturday next."

"I imagine a great many people are interested in the race." Eric wished the man would be out with whatever he wanted. He must be an agent of the person – or persons – who held the remainder of his father's debt. Come to make sure he understood the stakes, hence bringing along the muscle.

"Indeed. And a great many people have placed bets. Especially on your Mercury." The man paused while the barkeep brought their drinks. He took one sip of the wine, made a face, and set it back down on the roughly made table. His companion knocked back his whiskey without blinking.

"It has come to my employer's attention that you are in want of funds. Rather desperately, some would say."

A new thought had entered Eric's mind and his stomach turned at the prospect. These men weren't from his debt collectors. "And what concern is that to your employer?"

"If perhaps your horse were to place, or even show … there could still be considerable financial gain for you in the outcome of the race."

Cheating. They wanted him to purposefully lose the race.

Eric felt anger starting to rise. He leaned forward over the table, his fist coming down hard on the thick oak tabletop. "Who sent you?"

A smile curved up the tweed-man's lips. The beast beside him made an ominous snort. "No need for temper, my lord."

"What you are suggesting is outrageous." Eric had heard enough, he got to his feet intending to storm from the pub.

"Perhaps you will not think so when you consider this." The tweed-man reached into his inner breast pocket and removed a neatly folded piece of paper, which he slid across the table to Eric. Eric stared at it as if it was poisoned. "Look at it," the man urged.

Not sitting back down, Eric picked up the paper from the table, holding it with the same care one might handle an explosive. He unfolded it. Just one thing was written on the parchment.

"What is this?"

"The amount that will be settled upon you should you decide to accept my employer's offer."

One Race to Ruin 131

Eric's grip on the paper tightened, it wrinkled in his hand. It was an amount he could hardly begin to fathom. Enough to repay all of his father's debts. Enough for him to start investing and rebuilding the stable into a solvent enterprise. But the cost of doing such a thing was more than monetary.

He shook his head definitively. "I cannot."

The tweed-man shrugged as if it was neither here nor there to him. He stood up and his hulking companion followed suit. "Think it over, my lord." He inclined his head towards the crumpled paper still in Eric's hand. "Hold on to that while you contemplate. If you wish to speak to us more —"

"I won't —"

"We will be around."

It had the ring of a threat disguised as a promise. The two men turned towards the door, then the smaller put his hand on the bigger man's arm to pause him. The tweed-man turned back towards Eric. "Of course, there is also the matter of a certain exercise rider in your employ."

What little color was left in Eric's face drained instantly. The smaller man quirked the right corner of his mouth slightly, the only hint of satisfaction that showed.

Eric cleared his throat, his voice hard and gruff. "Your concern is with me and me alone."

The other corner of the man's mouth curved into a smile. "We should very much like it to stay that way." He inclined his head and then followed his brutish companion out the door of the tavern.

Eric sank back down onto the bench, the numbness that had taken over his body slowly giving way to tingling. Painful tingling. Worry. Fear. And now, not just for himself.

Chapter 15

Thursday was bittersweet for Dani. It would be her last ride on Mercury and her last day as an exercise rider for Eric. She felt confident that Mercury would win on Saturday. He was too good not to. And he would go on to race in the Derby and St. Ledger. But she would not be his rider anymore. The near miss with Kenner had convinced her of what Eric had tried to from the moment he discovered her secret identity – they were on borrowed time. The longer she kept at it the more likely someone was to discover her. If Mercury won the 2000 Guineas, the attention and scrutiny would only increase.

Eric caught her eye as soon as she emerged from the stable. The look on his face was heated; he certainly no longer saw her as just Dani the exercise boy. And he was so much more than the gruff and grumpy owner of a difficult horse. She would miss seeing him every day.

He fell into step beside her, their boots crunching across the dry ground. It had been an unusually dry spring and the turf beneath their feet did not have any of its characteristic squelch.

"I regret that this will be the last time I will see you in breeches," Eric said boldly.

Dani could not believe those words had just come out of his mouth. She looked over at him, surprised and warmed to see the smile on his face. He was handsome even with that stern expression she had come to know so well. But when he smiled … it was completely disarming.

"I will be here tomorrow, you know. Mr. Taylor said we were to keep this prince happy and on routine. I thought I'd come and give him a good brush tomorrow morning." Although her words were casual, her heart was pounding in its chest. She craved his touch, the moment he would hand her up into the saddle, his strong, capable hands upon her.

"It is probably for the best. We cannot go on like this."

This time, Dani chuckled. "And why not?"

"Because if one more person catches me making eyes at the exercise boy, I am going to get a certain kind of reputation."

Daniela clucked her tongue. "Such judgment. I would not have thought you so conservative —"

He gritted his teeth. How did she manage to put him at ease and also rile him up at the exact same time? "I do not begrudge a man his pleasures nor judge what he does behind the privacy of closed doors," he responded. "What I do object to is being mischaracterized when all I want to do is drag you off the bloody horse and teach you a damn thing or two."

She pursed her lips. Lord, how could they look any fuller? "What exactly is it you want to teach me?" Daniela breathed, pouting out those beautiful rose-colored lips.

"You ready, lad?" Taylor interrupted them.

For once, Dani was not the one who flushed. Eric's entire face flooded a bright reddish pink. Dani had to push down the gleeful smile that threatened to take over her face. "I am ready, sir. Nice and easy today."

"Nice and easy," Taylor confirmed. He frowned at Eric. "Are you alright, Fordham?"

Eric sputtered, putting his hand to his mouth as if to cover a coughing fit. "I am fine," he managed to bite out.

"Alright, then. Up you go, Dani-boy." Taylor stepped up and offered his hands to help Dani into the saddle.

A quick pulse of disappointment flashed through her; she glanced at Eric, seeing the matching sentiment on his face. But then there was no more time to think. She was in the saddle, and Mercury, as always, required her full attention.

"Take him the full mile. A trot the first half, a canter the third quarter, and then open him up for the last stretch. That's it. Then come on back," Taylor instructed.

"Yes, sir," Dani nodded and loosened her grip on the reins, urging Mercury forward. Eric and Taylor started walking towards the rail. Since this wasn't a timed run, they were going to wait for Dani and Mercury there rather than walking down to the finish line.

Greene joined them a minute or so later at the rail.

"How's he looking today?" Greene asked.

"Fit and fine, as always. You can ride him back to stables at a walk, just so he continues to be comfortable with you aboard." Taylor took out and lit his pipe as he spoke.

"Fine, fine," Greene nodded. "How's Red Falcon running?"

"Clocked a good time yesterday," Eric put in.

"Not good enough," Taylor opined, puffing out a ring of smoke. "They've got Stevenson aboard. He's conservative, no matter how you tell him to ride –"

"Something's wrong." Eric was already halfway onto the track.

Mercury was cantering backward down the middle of the turf, riderless.

"What the –"

"Not again –"

"There's no saddle –"

Eric took off at a run. He didn't even think about the horse; someone would catch him. A new vision of Dani had entered his mind. A very ugly one. The words of the tweed-clad man from the tavern echoed in his head.

Then it wasn't just a vision. It was real. She was hunched on the ground, Mercury's saddle a few yards away on the turf. Eric fell to his knees beside her.

"Are you alright? What happened?"

"He's just had the wind knocked out of him, he'll be alright," another exercise rider said, crouched on Dani's other side.

Dani was sputtering and coughing, trying to catch her breath. Eric put his arm around her shoulders.

"You're alright," he said softly. The other man gave him a strange look.

"The saddle came loose," Dani managed to say between ragged breaths.

"How can that be?" Eric looked around, his arm still tight around her shoulders. Greene and Taylor were approaching. Greene held Mercury's bridle firmly in his hand. Taylor scooped up the saddle, examining it as he walked towards them.

"Someone's cut the girth strap –"

"What?" Dani's head whipped around in surprise, and the cap, already loosened from her fall to the ground, fell from her head. It landed on the green turf unceremoniously.

Freed from their prison, her bright red curls caught and shone in the sun. The exercise rider who had kneeled beside her gasped and jumped back as if burned.

"Who – a woman?" He sputtered.

"Daniela?" Greene nearly dropped his hold on Mercury. "Daniela, have ye lost yer damn mind, girl?" He stammered, realizing that he did indeed recognize the young woman before him.

Dani's eyes rose to meet Eric's. *"Lo siento,"* she murmured.

"Dani, wait –" Eric tried to stop her, but she shrugged off his arm and climbed to her feet.

With as much dignity as she could, she walked away from the growing group of onlookers. She did not bother replacing her cap. Word of what had happened would spread through the racing community with the ferocity of a wildfire. Eventually, it would reach her aunt, and there would be hell to pay.

Eric watched her go with his heart in his throat. He wanted to go after her, to protect her from the scorn and gossip. But he knew as well as anyone there would be no preventing what was to come. The scandal would rock Newmarket and its sister city, Cambridge. It would be discussed in London; first in the Jockey Club, then in the other gentleman's clubs that lined Pall Mall, and finally in the halls and ballrooms of the London *haute ton*. And nothing he could say or do at this point would prevent that from happening.

He could marry her. The thought popped into his mind unbidden. Before he could process that new notion, he felt a tap on his shoulder.

Eric climbed to his feet to face Taylor and Greene. The trainer and jockey on whom his only hope of rebuilding his family fortunes now hung. He tried to quickly prepare himself for the worst.

"Someone cut the strap." Taylor held up the offending item to show them. "See the underside here? The cut is clean. Made by something sharp like a knife. But the last half-inch or so is torn, ripped. Someone cut the strap almost all the way through and then let the stress from the tightened girth and the ride finish the job."

Eric took the mangled saddle from Taylor's hands, examining the broken leather strap for himself.

"It's a lucky thing that it was just an easy run today. If she'd opened him up for a full gallop …" Greene shook his head, rubbing his hand over this grizzled, stubbly chin. "She always was a damnably willful little hoyden."

"She could have died," Eric stammered, his insides hardening into something much darker.

The three men stood silently. Taylor fiddled with his pipe. Greene examined the saddle. Eric stared at the ground. Then he had a realization. He started to scan the crowd. Sure enough, he found what – or rather, who – he was looking for almost immediately.

Bradford Kenner stood a few yards back from the rail talking casually to two other men that Eric vaguely recognized. Probably staff in Kenner's racing operation. Kenner's hands were in his pockets, his stance nonchalant. But his face wore a deeply satisfied look.

But that was not all Eric saw. Fifteen yards away, near the gap in fencing where horses were being brought between the different training grounds, loomed a huge, hulking figure. His companion, the neatly-dressed tweed-man with the thick mustache, was nowhere in sight. But the message was clear enough.

He did not know who had done it, but it did not matter. He was going to –

"Did you know?" Greene asked directly, the saddle hanging limp at his side and a look that said he expected to be answered on his face.

Eric nodded. "Not at the beginning. When I discovered it, I tried to stop her."

"Unsuccessfully," Taylor observed drolly.

"Aye, well, Daniela Rames has a mind all her own," Greene put in with a shake of his head.

"Rames?" Taylor asked from under raised eyebrows.

"Yes, that Rames. Daughter of Nathanial Rames. I can't believe I did not recognize her; I've known the girl since she was in nappies." Greene held up the saddle, his eyes clouded. "I'm mighty thankful not to be breaking much darker news to her father."

"Well, no surprise she could ride." As Taylor spoke, Mercury nosed at the trainer's shoulder, reminding them all that he too was still here. And his favorite rider was gone. "Tomorrow we rest Mercury. Then on Saturday, we'll make our run. There's nothing else to do."

Eric could not have disagreed more. There was plenty to do and he wanted to do it now, with his fists. He clenched his hands tightly at his sides, his knuckles white. Beside him, Greene and Taylor exchanged looks. It was not difficult to read the murderous look in the Earl of Fordham's eyes.

Greene was not a big man but he was strong, used to handling forty stone, finicky thoroughbreds. He gripped Eric's left arm hard. Taylor, now holding Mercury's rein, took a subtler but comparatively forceful approach. He moved to place himself between Eric and the growing crowd.

"They're watching you, lad. If you react, they all will. We will get to the bottom of this. But nothing will be solved by having it out here and now. Except to put Mercury at risk."

His insides were raging as hot as a forest fire. If Kenner had done this, he would tear him to shreds. The man was half his size. Eric had not engaged in fisticuffs since he was at school, but he was confident he could take apart the cowardly, conniving man … But what if it had not been Kenner? That thought burned even more. If it had not been Kenner, if the tweed-man and his companion were responsible — then so was Eric. For not protecting her. And he would be damned if he would risk her getting hurt again.

It took every measure of control that Eric had. And the forceful presence of the two other men at his side and front. Still, it almost wasn't enough.

Eric grabbed the bridle away from Taylor and stalked off in the opposite direction. He would take the long way around back to the stables. And hopefully leading his last, best hope of salvation, the demanding chestnut beast, would keep him from doing anything rash along the way.

Chapter 16

Daniela did not bother changing her clothes or sneaking in through the servant's quarters. She rode her horse directly into the stable yard, her long red hair now unpinned and flowing freely down her shoulders.

Recognizing her despite her getup, a stable boy came forward to take the reins of the horse. He offered her a hand down as he would always do to a young lady of the house, though he kept his eyes carefully downcast.

The head groom emerged from the small stable and came to an immediate halt. His mouth fell open. "Miss Rames ..."

"She's had a long, fast ride from Newmarket," Daniela said briskly, handing over control of the steady mare she had ridden out that morning. "Walk her out and given her a good rub down."

"Of course, miss," the groom answered.

Daniela paid him no more attention. Since the moment she'd realized her identity was discovered and her ruse was over, she'd known exactly what she needed to do. No further thoughts had entered her mind. She could not let them or she would lose her nerve.

She walked up the front steps of the house, feeling the eyes of the stable hands and grooms upon her. She did not knock. Inside the foyer, the maid who was refilling water in the vases from a large pitcher nearly dropped the aforementioned pitcher on the thick Turkish rug.

But Daniela marched past the young servant into the parlor, where she knew she would find her aunt and cousin having their afternoon tea.

Today, her Uncle Baxter was with them as well. Millie and Baxter were seated on the chintz-patterned sofa. Her uncle was taking hearty bites of a scone laden heavily with jam while her aunt stirred her steaming cup of tea. Winnie was reaching across the tea tray to set the little saucer of cream back down after tipping a bit into her teacup.

Winnie saw Daniela first. Her hand froze in midair, a few pearly white drops of cream sloshing out of the saucer and onto the silver tea tray. Millie made a little *tsk* sound at her daughter's clumsiness as she stirred. Baxter and Millie turned to face their niece at the same time, though their faces could not have looked much more different.

Uncle Baxter's face went blank, as if he could not process the sight in front of him. Conversely, his wife's face showed a parade of emotions – shock, anger, disdain, and finally satisfaction. She had known all along that this niece of hers was destined for ruin; now she was validated.

"Aunt, Uncle," Daniela dipped a little curtsey before continuing as if she were wearing an ordinary muslin day dress rather than breeches, a rough-hewn linen shirt, and a tweed vest. "For the last month or so, I have spent my mornings working as an exercise rider at the Newmarket training grounds. I have been in the employ of the Earl of Fordham. He and his staff were completely unaware of my identity or gender. However, precipitous events have unfolded such that my status is now publicly known."

Not wanting to give them any time to respond — well, really just her Aunt Millie — Daniela gave a definitive nod and turned for the door.

"You will give up this masquerade immediately," Millie said sharply, halting her niece halfway to the door.

Daniela felt her chest tighten painfully. Every beat of her heart felt like the repeated touching of a bruise. "On that, Aunt Millie, we are regrettably agreed."

Then she turned on her heel and left the room as quickly as her feet would carry her.

Daniela changed her clothing without calling for a maid. She ripped her exercise rider's costume from her body with such ferocity, a button bounced across the floor and rolled under the big four-poster bed. She went to the armoire, pulled out the first dress her hand touched, and yanked it into place over her head. She

One Race to Ruin

had to twist her arms behind her painfully to fasten all of the buttons but she appreciated the discomfort. When she was finally dressed as befitting a young lady, she sat down at the compact desk in the corner of her room. She pulled out parchment and quill pen and started to write.

It did not take Daniela long to finish her missive. Her message to her father was simple: she needed to come home, regardless of the progress or lack thereof her father had made in mending his reputation. And she needed to come home now.

She pushed back her chair with such force it nearly overturned. She caught it with her hand just in time to tip it back into place. *No need to cause any more commotion than she already had.* Daniela laughed aloud at the absurdity of her own thought.

As she neatly folded the letter, the pile of clothing at the foot of her bed caught her eye. It was a mangled mess – a perfect analogy for her life right at this moment.

However, she found herself setting the letter aside and leaning down. She carefully, almost lovingly, picked up each article of clothing, folding and setting them in a neat pile on the little bench at the end of her bed. If only her life could be restored to order with such carefully applied attentions. She sighed deeply.

She must send the letter to her father immediately. With any luck, she could be on the coach to Gainsborough by the week end.

Dani picked up the letter and headed for the door.

"Where do you think you are going?"

Startled by the harsh voice the moment her feet touched the ground floor landing, Daniela nearly tripped on the hemline of her day dress. She turned around to find her Aunt Millie standing in the doorway between the foyer and the parlor. Her arms were crossed across her body and she wore a deep frown.

"I am going to post a letter to my father," Daniela said slowly.

"You are not to leave this house."

"What?" She blinked twice, as if she was not seeing things clearly.

"You are confined to the premises. I'd prefer you not even go outside, where the neighbors might see you. But I suppose even I must have some compassion." Millie's face hardly changed as she spoke.

"Compassion?" Daniela echoed in disbelief.

"Give the letter to me. I will see it posted." Millie held out her hand expectantly.

Daniela clutched the folded quarto tighter in her hand. "I should like to post it myself, to see it safely on its way."

"Are you suggesting that I would not post your letter?"

"I am just saying –"

"You have said, *and done*, quite enough already."

"Aunt Millie, I –"

"What is going on?" Winnie appeared at the top of the stairs. She took one look at her mother and cousin staring each other down from across the entry hall and hurried down the steps. "Mother?"

It was Daniela who answered. "I am not allowed to leave the house."

Winnie's eyebrows shot up. She turned to her mother. "What does she mean?"

One Race to Ruin 147

The older woman's face did not soften. She looked sternly at her daughter. "This is none of your concern, Winnie. I won't have you worrying about it. The Lord knows, this wild child has done enough to your reputation. Off with you."

"Mother, you can hardly keep her locked up —"

"She has ruined you, Winnie. Do you not understand that?" The volume of Millie's voice increased, the tone turning shrill as she threw infuriated looks between her daughter and niece. "Upstairs with you, with both of you." Millie waved her hand and turned to go back into the parlor.

"She hasn't ruined me."

Aunt Millie turned back towards them slowly. She looked confused. Like she could not figure out where the voice had come from. Daniela felt a rush of affection for her cousin.

"Mother, I —"

"You do not know what you are talking about, Winnie." Millie had recovered from her surprise. She pointed her finger at her niece emphatically. "Once word of this gets to London there will be no invitations, no callers. Winnie will be completely bereft and it is your —"

"Mama!"

Millie looked directly at her daughter this time, a mix of shock and fury on her face.

"I've no need to go to London again. Mr. Rayden has asked my permission to ask Papa for my hand, and I have told him yes," Winnie explained. She was wringing her hands, but a hopeful little smile curved up the corners of her mouth.

"Mr. Rayden?" Aunt Millie shook her head in disbelief. She rounded on Daniela. "See what you've done? You have filled her head with fanciful notions, thinking she can marry down like that! She should be matched with an earl or a marquess!"

"How is any of this my fault?" Daniela was shaking her head, completely disbelieving what was happening around her.

"You have been masquerading as a man! You have been spending time – *unchaperoned* – with a gentleman who has a reputation in London for chasing skirts! Just your presence in this house brings shame upon every one of us! God only knows what you have actually done –"

"I haven't done anything! I have not ruined my reputation, I am not compromised –" Though as she said those words, she could not help remembering the long kiss she had shared with Eric on the terrace of Lady St. Marten's soiree.

"It does not matter what you have or haven't done, you stupid girl!" Millie was yelling now, advancing across the foyer towards her niece. She looked as if she might strike Daniela.

"That is enough, Mildred!"

Uncle Baxter strode across the room, taking his wife's arm firmly in his hand. "You will not raise a hand to my brother's daughter. She has been entrusted to our care, and I owe my brother that much. Even if we have not been able to see her truly safe from … ruin." He sighed.

For the first time, Dani felt a rush of shame.

Her aunt looked stricken that her husband would speak to or handle her so. Millie opened her mouth to respond but Daniela did not stick around to hear it. She rushed for the stairs, her letter safe in her hand. For the first time, tears started to fall. They burned her eyes as she stumbled up the stairs and down the hall to her bedroom.

The gravity of what had happened in the last twenty-four hours came crashing down on her like a pile of bricks. She wanted it to all go away. She wanted to go home to her father. She wanted to feel warm, comforting arms around her: Eric's arms.

As the sobs wrenched her body, Daniela did not hear the door open. But when she felt the tentative touch on her shoulder she knew who it was.

Winnie rubbed her back. She did not try to talk to her or offer empty words of solace. She just moved her hand methodically up and down Daniela's back as her shoulders shook.

When Daniela's sobs had finally softened into slow-rolling tears, Winnie reached out and delicately pulled the crumpled letter from between Daniela's fingers.

"I will post your letter for you," she said softly.

Daniela drew a very unsteady breath. She leaned back against her cousin, who received her with open arms. "Thank you, Winnie."

Chapter 17

Eric debated whether he should come. He could not discuss it with anyone. Greene and Taylor had been uncommonly understanding about the whole debacle but neither knew the depth of involvement between Eric and Daniela. And it must stay that way if he was not to irrevocably damage her reputation and prospects.

Perhaps he would be able to reason with Baxter Rames, to help him see that the situation was not as bad as it seemed on first examination. *Hell, it was worse.*

But no one other than he and Daniela knew that.

And to Daniela … what would he say?

He lifted his hand to knock on the door before he lost his nerve to do anything at all. But before his hand could connect the door swung open. Instead of standing face to face with a well-dressed footman or butler, he had to look downward. He recognized

Daniela's cousin immediately, though he could not have recalled her name.

"Miss Rames, I –"

"Hush!" The blonde Miss Rames admonished him brusquely. She put up her hand, signaling him to wait while she looked back over her shoulder. "Come, quickly."

She opened the door and ushered him in, shutting it behind her as quietly as she could. Eric opened his mouth to question her but she shook her head sharply, hurrying off as soon as the door was safely closed.

Eric followed her through the entry hall, across a well-appointed formal parlor, past a heavy wooden door that connected to a small library and into an alcove with tall glass windows. Almost like a miniature conservatory tucked into this remote corner of the house.

"Stay here," she instructed, starting to leave the way they had come.

"I wish to speak with your parents, Miss Rames – the other Miss Rames' – uncle and aunt –"

"That is a terrible idea," Winnie said emphatically. Eric raised his dark eyebrows. "Stay here. I will go and fetch Daniela. And for the love of God, be quiet!"

She disappeared back into the main library and then the parlor. Eric got a very uncomfortable feeling in the pit of his stomach. *A terrible idea*, she'd said. That did not bode well for his chances of helping Daniela's cause. *Dani's* cause. Eric had spent time getting to know both sides of the young woman. And he felt deeply connected to both of them.

What would he say to her? He was sorry, certainly. But for what?

For discovering her identity in the first place? For allowing the charade to go on? For getting her mixed up with the deplorable likes of Bradford Kenner and those dangerous men who may well have tried to kill her?

For kissing her?

Her cousin was fast on her feet for not two minutes later she reappeared, this time with his red-haired vision on her heels. Eric's heart thumped louder in his chest just being in the same room with her. *How had she managed to inspire these intense feelings in him in such a short span of time?* They'd known each other for hardly a month.

"I'll leave the door from the parlor to the library open so Mother cannot accuse you of any more impropriety."

Daniela grasped her hands tightly. "You're a dear, Winnie."

Winnie squeezed back. "I will keep watch in the parlor."

And then they were alone.

"I am so sorry —"

"Eric, I cannot —"

Despite the terrible circumstances, they both chuckled. "Please, go ahead."

"I am sorry for not taking the threat of Kenner more seriously. He must have seen me the other day. And now, everything that you have worked for — Mercury, the 2000 Guineas, Mr. Taylor and Mr. Greene ..." Dani shook her head mournfully, her gaze dropping to the ground. "I am just so sorry."

Eric breathed in and out. In and out. Again. She heard each breath, long and drawn out. Then she felt his hand touch hers. Her eyes snapped up to meet his.

"This is my fault. I should have stopped this charade the moment I discovered it."

Dani nodded sadly. "If you had, you would not be the center of such a scandal. I was thinking only of myself –"

"No, Dani. *I was thinking only of myself.* I am … I am afraid that I am not the only one who will be ruined by this scandal." As he spoke, he took her smaller hand into his, gripping it hard. She returned the grasp, her strong fingers holding tightly to his own.

"My aunt certainly seems to agree with you. She has forbidden me from leaving the house." Despite the agony of the past several hours the warmth that spread from their joined hands brought her an inexplicable amount of peace. She found herself praying that he would not come to his senses and draw his hand away.

Eric grimaced. "Perhaps if I spoke with your uncle. Your cousin seems to think it is a lost cause, but …"

Dani shook her head. "Despite his affection for my father, my Uncle Baxter agrees with my aunt. I am ruined," she said simply.

"How can you say it so lightly?"

"Because it does not mean to me what it does to them. All I want is to go home."

The words hurt him more than he had expected. She did not want him. A part of him had expected … well, he had expected her to tell him they ought to be married. That her reputation was compromised and the only way to salvage it would be if they were wed. And of course, he had been prepared to tell her all the reasons why that could not be so.

But she did not ask. She did not even insinuate.

She did not want him. All she wanted was to go home.

He withdrew his hand. Dani wanted to grab it back. She opened her mouth to say more but Winnie's footsteps interrupted them.

"She's coming!"

Dani's stomach clenched tight. Eric steeled himself for the encounter, pushing his feelings for Dani down as the older woman swept in on Winnie's heels.

"My lord! I am most alarmed to find you here. My husband has always held your family in such high regard –"

"I appreciate that, Mrs. Rames. I would very much like to speak with your husband –"

"That is not possible." Millie crossed her arms and shook her head. Although she was a head shorter than Eric and tiny in build by comparison, she was a stalwart foe. "Mr. Rames has gone out for the evening."

Eric was undeterred. He was the Earl of Fordham. "Then perhaps you and I should speak, Mrs. Rames. I am under the impression that you consider your niece's reputation to be ruined."

"And it is you who have done the ruining," Millie said flatly. "Have you come here to propose marriage?"

Dani gasped. Such a thing had not even crossed her mind.

"I have not," Eric said tightly. His hands curled into fists at his side.

Dani felt her heart drop. In an instant, she had seen a future flash before her eyes: her, Eric, an estate brimming with horses and children. But his three words, spoken with such visible discomfort, had darkened the vision as efficiently as a window shade.

"Then there is nothing more to be said here, my lord," Millie said, the self-satisfied look Dani had first seen that afternoon returning.

Eric looked hard at the older woman, but she would not be chastened by him. He turned to Dani, who stood where he had left her moments before. Though where their hands had been joined in unity, she now held her own tightly in front of her.

"Dani – Miss Rames, I –"

"I think you had best go, Lord Fordham," Dani said quietly.

The nervousness in his stomach turned to something colder, more disappointed. And hurt. He bowed very awkwardly to Dani and then walked past Winnie and her mother without acknowledgment. He was thankful it was a direct route out of the house.

His chest was tightening, each breath a struggle for air. By the time he burst outside onto the doorstep he had to grip the stone railing for support. It seemed impossible; if someone had asked him on his way to the Rames' household how much worse the situation could get, he might have laughed aloud at them. And yet, the weight of disappointment and regret upon his chest had grown. He was nearly suffocating.

Chapter 18

The next morning was cloudy and cold. The warm, dry weather that had buoyed them through the first few weeks of the season seemed to be deserting now. As Eric stood at the rail watching his horses at the morning workouts, he felt the first few droplets of rain start to fall on his cheeks and shoulders.

He had not slept. He had not anticipated the change in weather. He was cold, tired, and grumpy.

His trainer stood at the rail next to him watching the horses cross the finish line, clicking his stopwatch. Scribbling down times on a little scrap of paper. Several others stood around them watching the training runs. Dynasty thundered past. Taylor clicked his stopwatch and made an approving noise.

Two men near them spoke in elevated whispers.

One Race to Ruin

"Not a bad time. Wonder if he's got another lass aboard."

"I hope you didn't already place your bet on the 2000 Guineas."

Eric's whole body stiffened.

"Fordham! Did you see my horse come in? Quite pleased with that time." Bradford Kenner stopped midstride, walking beside his own trainer. He smiled widely. Eric said nothing. "Of course, with a proper rider aboard myriad things are possible …" Kenner trailed off as he resumed walking.

"Ignore them."

Eric kept his eyes trained forward as Taylor took another puff from his pipe.

"They aren't wrong."

Taylor made only a nondescript *hrmph* sound.

"I knew what was going on and I let her continue with the charade. Because I was too damn worried about saving my own skin."

"Sounds like you feel guilty rather than angry."

Eric sighed. "Does it matter?"

"That depends. Whose opinions do you care about?"

That was the question. Because Eric was hearing the opinions of the English horseracing scene loud and clear. He had not been out to any social gatherings, but Daniela's aunt had said enough to give him an idea of exactly what was going to be said in those circles. What he did not have a clear picture of was how Daniela felt … or how he felt about it himself, once all the interference was cleared away.

Guilt? Yes, that was there in spades. He should have protected Daniela from this ridicule. He should have insisted she stop the moment he had discovered her masquerade, no matter the cost to him. He could lose all hopes of restoring his family fortune, that was true. But Daniela … she had lost all hope of a happy future. Finding a husband, having a family, helping her father restore his good name … all of that would come to naught. She could have lost her life. And while of course, she bore responsibility for her own choices, Eric could not deny the part he had played.

"Mercury has as good a chance of winning tomorrow as he's ever had," Taylor opined.

"Not if this rain continues." Eric looked up at the sky, which was turning a darker ominous gray by the minute.

"Better, than if the woman had never shown up," Taylor continued.

"You think I should be thanking her."

"Don't you?"

"I don't know."

"That woman is the reason your horse is ready to run tomorrow." Taylor pulled his pipe out of his mouth and turned to look directly at the earl. "Tatum told me what happened when you went to recruit him. That she was the one – albeit not as herself – to convince him to come on board."

Eric nodded. "She was, indeed."

"Well, it's like you said. You ought to be thanking the woman instead of apologizing to her. For her."

"If Mercury doesn't win tomorrow we will never be taken seriously again. No one will ride for us. No one will want to breed with our stock. We'll be priced out of every yearling sale. I will have to sell my father's house in Cambridge. And every horse in the racing string. It will be over." Eric had never said the words aloud. Not so plainly.

One Race to Ruin

"Might be."

The two men stood in silence then. They watched as the last two horses that Taylor had scheduled for that morning made their run. Then they walked together back towards the stable, silence still reigning between them.

As they reached the stable yard the head groom came forward. At his side was a boy who could not have been more than thirteen or fourteen years old. Eric vaguely recalled having seen him mucking stalls.

"Pardon me, my lord, sir." The head groom nodded to Eric and Taylor. "Ye asked me to question the employees. This lad here, he had something interesting to say."

He nudged the boy forward but the young man looked incredibly nervous. He had probably never spoken directly to anyone who held a noble title. Let alone to the head trainer. He was fiddling with the frayed ends of his braided-twine belt.

"Yes?"

"Tell them what ye saw, boy."

"Well, I'm not that sure, ye see. It was early. Just dawn … and, well, I was mighty sleepy …"

The head groom rolled his eyes, tired of waiting for the lad. "He saw a man in the stable when he first arrived for his morning chores. Leaving the tack room."

"The tack room?" *Where the saddles were kept.* Eric felt his pulse quicken. "What did this man look like?"

"He was very tall, sir. Not just tall … I mean – he was tall, but … big."

"He was a very big fellow?" Taylor clarified.

The boy nodded solemnly.

Taylor glanced over at Eric. Although Eric thought his face was neutral, Taylor must have read something there for he did not push the boy for more details.

"Alright, back to your chores." The head groom sent the boy on his way then turned back to Taylor and Eric.

"Have you found anything else? What about the Kenner chap?" Taylor asked. He had picked up on the subtext of Kenner's comments earlier that morning.

The groom shrugged. "Kenner's always around. His stable block is only two down from ours. No one saw anything out of the ordinary, but …"

"But he still had ample opportunity to tamper with the saddle," Eric finished.

The big man that the stable boy had described could be the same hulking brute that had tried to intimidate Eric into compromising the race and had subtly threatened Dani. Or it could have been someone hired by Kenner to see the deed done. Or the sleepy lad might have been dreaming and Kenner had damaged the saddle at some other time. They were not actually any closer to determining the culprit.

"The boy's words meant something to you," Taylor said quietly as the head groom retreated towards the stable block.

"Yes." Eric sighed. "But not enough."

"Do you think Mercury is in any danger?"

Eric shook his head. "No. This is about me."

"Even so, I think I'll have the lads take it in rounds to patrol the stables tonight. Just to be safe." Taylor glanced up at Eric. Finding no argument, he set off to see it done.

Eric rubbed his hand over his chin. He hadn't shaved that morning and a day's worth of dark stubble shadowed his chin. *Just fine.* It matched his mood.

The rain turned from a steady drizzle to a downpour.

Chapter 19

Dani watched the rain outside her window with growing anxiety. It would make the roads difficult. Especially after such a long dry spell. There would be flooding. Wheels would get stuck in deep puddles. Horses would tire faster and have to be changed out sooner. The post would be delayed. And her letter to her father – faithfully posted by her dear cousin the evening before – might not reach him for days. Even a week, if he had not made it back to Gainsborough by now.

It was too long. The situation with her aunt was completely intolerable. Since Eric's visit Daniela could scarcely leave her room without being berated. And if her aunt was silent, she was looking down her nose at Daniela with that horribly superior, self-satisfied sneer upon her face.

One Race to Ruin

She had to go. Daniela went to the armoire and started pulling out dresses. She would not be able to manage a trunk. The shoulder bag she'd been using to hide her outfit changes would have to suffice. She packed quickly, stuffing gowns and undergarments and accessories into the bag without regard for folding. She had almost all of the pocket money her father had given her when she departed Gainsborough months before, plus the money she'd been paid for riding Mercury. She crossed to the little writing desk and pulled out the drawer, plucking up the coins and placing them into her drawstring reticule.

There was a knock at the door.

Daniela froze, the little velvet reticule crushed in her hand. She dropped it into the drawer and closed it with a *snap*. She took two steps back, tossed her shoulder bag onto the floor and kicked it under the bed.

"Come in!" She called.

Her breath whooshed out of her like a gust of wind when Winnie poked her head in rather than her Aunt Millie.

"Winnie," she breathed. "Come in, come in."

Winnie closed the door quietly behind her. Daniela turned back to the desk, pulling the reticule out of the drawer and dropping it on the wood surface. Then she leaned down and retrieved her bag from under the bed.

"You're leaving," Winnie said grimly. It was not a question.

Daniela nodded. "I can't stay here, Winnie."

"Take me with you?"

Daniela laughed despite her internal agony. "If only I could." She reached over and squeezed her cousin's hand.

"Where will you go?"

"Back home. I should never have come to Cambridge."

Winnie looked out the window dubiously. "Don't you think you could wait until tomorrow? Surely the rain will have cleared by then."

It was a tempting thought. The rain was coming down in unrelenting sheets. The fact that venturing out into that melee seemed the better option spoke loudly about the deterioration of her circumstances in her aunt and uncle's home.

"I meant to ask you, Winnie … was what you said about Mr. Rayden true? Has he asked for your hand?"

Winnie smiled shyly. She nodded, her blonde curls bouncing prettily.

A genuine smile warmed Daniela's face. "I am so happy for you."

"You don't think I am marrying down?"

Daniela rolled her eyes. "I think you know how I feel about your mother's opinions." Impulsively, she pulled Winnie into a tight hug. When she pulled back she held her at arm's length. "Wait until things have calmed down and then go directly to your father. I think Uncle Baxter will come through for you."

"You truly think so?"

"I do."

"Mr. Rayden will not be bothered by all of this scandal Mama is so concerned about," Winnie said confidently.

One Race to Ruin 165

"Of course, he won't. He knows a prize when he sees it." Dani hugged Winnie tightly again. This time when she drew back her smile had faded. "I must go."

Winnie did not argue now. "What shall I tell Mother and Father?"

"The truth. Tell them I've gone home." A smile tugged at the corner of Daniela's lips. "Perhaps just don't tell them right away."

Winnie smiled conspiratorially. "Oh no. I think tonight you are taking supper in your room. I'm certain that's what I overheard the maids saying."

"You're a dear."

"Do you have a way out?"

Daniela chuckled. "I have gotten very good at sneaking out of this house."

It wasn't just raining. It was like a tropical monsoon – of course, those did not happen in England, and Eric had never traveled far enough to have witnessed one himself. But this was exactly how he pictured it: the unseasonably warm weather had returned through the afternoon and evening, but instead of sunshine there was a never-ending downpour.

Mercury had never run in conditions like this. The spring had been so clear, occasionally overcast, a drizzle here and there. All of the serious training they had done in the past few months had been in essentially ideal racing conditions. But tomorrow morning the Rowley Mile would be sloppy and wet. Mud would fling back from the hooves of the leaders, covering the rest of the pack in the muck. Some horses excelled on the wet track, but only tomorrow would tell if Mercury was one of them.

Eric was watching the rainfall with a kind of detached blankness. He could not feel anything more. He felt like a towel that had been dunked and then wrung out repeatedly. The last week had squeezed out every bit of energy he had left.

He had poured himself a drink but it sat untended on the windowsill next to where his booted feet were propped up. He'd cracked open the window a few inches so he could hear the sound of the raindrops hitting the stonework outside.

How much longer would he live here? He started to wonder. But that depended on tomorrow.

Eric had come home to this house almost every day of his life. He had tripped and skinned his knees on the front steps where the rain now pattered down melodically. He'd once tied the reins of a temperamental horse around the ornately carved twin equine statues that flanked the stairs. He'd felt his father's wrath when said horse had decapitated one of the stone steeds.

In someplace deep in his mind, not even quite conscious, Eric had envisioned holding his own son's hand as they climbed those very stone stairs. And now, all of those visions of past and present stood to be lost.

Eric was determined to etch the memories on his brain so that no matter what happened tomorrow he might have something to hold onto. He closed his eyes, so he could listen more fully to the sounds of the rain: the soft patter where it hit the stonework of the entryway, the louder plink where it intermittently struck the glass of the windows. He could not hear the water hitting the little rectangle of grass that separated the house from the street, but he could smell the distinct scent of wet greenery.

Then another sound permeated the steady, musical cadence.

Fast, then slow and steady, and then much quieter, the hesitant steps of a nervous hand at the reins. Hoofbeats. Then a long moment of peaceful rainfall. The crunch of boots on gravel. Footsteps – light, unsure, slow despite the downpour.

A decision made. Firmer steps … one, two, three, four … then at the landing. A split second and a sharp knock on the heavy, dark-stained oak door.

The butler emerged from the back of the house, a disgruntled look on his face. He would surely have been taking his evening tea down in the kitchen, waiting for Eric to go upstairs before turning in himself. But certainly, he had considered himself done for the night.

When he recalled the night later, Eric had no memory of coming to his feet, crossing the room, or intercepting the butler in the hall. He did not remember what words he said to the man as he dismissed him.

He only remembered opening the door, knowing with as much certainty who would be standing on his doorstep as he had uncertainty about the outcome of tomorrow's race.

Because who else could it be?

She was drenched. Every single part of her body was wet, right down to her petticoats and the freckled skin beneath. She'd been smart enough to wear a thick wool pelisse when she fled her aunt and uncle's house, but even that had not been enough against the ferocity of an English storm.

"May I come in?" Daniela was less than certain of her welcome after how they had left things last time they spoke.

Eric did not say anything but he stepped back into the entry hall and opened the door wider by way of answer.

She turned back towards the door. "My horse –"

"I've asked the butler to send for a groom to see him settled in the stable." Eric nodded towards the sitting room. "I've sent the staff to bed for the evening but I can build up the fire. You're shaking." Without waiting for her to acquiesce, he strode into the room, knelt before the grate, and went to work adding bigger logs from the holder on the left.

For once, Daniela did not argue. She followed him into the room, standing awkwardly on the corner of the hearthrug, dripping wet.

"You don't seem surprised to see me," Daniela observed to his back.

Eric sighed. "I think I have lost the capacity for any feelings at this point. But why are you out in this weather?"

One Race to Ruin

"I left my aunt and uncle's. I could not stay there a minute longer," she said bitterly.

"I can't say I begrudge you that sentiment." Eric stoked the fire with the poker, watching as the thick log he'd just placed caught flame.

"I left them a note saying I was returning home to my father."

"That's very thoughtful of you, considering your aunt's complete lack of regard or sympathy." He sat back on his heels, feeling the heat of the fire starting to permeate his own numbness.

"But I couldn't leave without seeing Mercury win."

Eric slowly came to his feet, like a large, graceful panther. He took two steps, his long legs bringing him to stand before her. His hands reached up and started undoing the buttons of her pelisse. "What will you do now?" He asked, even as his hands did the work of removing her sodden jacket. She could not possibly keep it on, he heard himself think. She was wet through.

"I tried to find lodging for the night. I have been looking for hours, but –"

"There is nothing to be found. Not during the spring meeting. Not the night before the 2000 Guineas." He unfastened the last button, tugged the jacket apart, and eased it over her shoulders. It fell in a wet heap on the rug behind her.

She was indeed soaked through. Her rose-colored muslin gown had turned a dark purple color where it was wet at the shoulders and neckline. She'd been wearing gloves when she came in, Eric thought somewhere deep in his mind. But she'd removed them between then and now because her strong, graceful hands peeked out from the wet ends of her sleeves. Her bright red hair was turned a darker shade by the rain, to a red tarnished bronze.

"I just could not bring myself to go back to my aunt and uncle's house. And then somehow, I ended up here." Daniela reached up and tucked back a stray curl. Eric's eyes followed the end of the wet tendril as it traveled up her breast, over her collarbone, along the delicate curve of her neck, and then down her back as she tucked it behind her ear.

Behind them, the newly deposited logs shifted within the fireplace, causing a new stream of flame and heat to rise up suddenly.

Eric caught the back of her neck in his hand and kissed the spot just below her ear where that perfect red curl had just been.

Despite the wetness of the muslin against her skin, all Daniela felt was heat. She stepped into his arms willingly. Perhaps she had known that by coming here, this was inevitable. Perhaps her heart had known it since that first time their lips touched behind the stables at Newmarket: that eventually they would be here, together, like this.

Then he took her lips.

He explored her slowly, the luxury of an empty house and a blazing fire giving him permission to take his time. This was not the back of a stable or a darkened terrace. Here they had complete privacy and no chance of being interrupted.

Eric traced her lips with his tongue from left to right and then back again. First the top, then the bottom, and then the top again. He wanted to know every inch of her sweet mouth.

When he deepened the kiss she welcomed him, eager to catch up to where they had been before.

One Race to Ruin

What she did not account for was the tantalizing effect his hands would have once they went to work.

They started at her waist. The fashionable empire-waisted gown skimmed her hips. He closed his hands around her so that he could feel her body beneath the fabric. His thumbs followed the downward slant of her hip bones, while his palms and fingers massaged the rounded flesh of her bottom. He was a large man while she had a rider's petite build. His wide hands covered her slim waist easily. But he did not keep them there.

Eric slid his hands upward. His thumbs felt the inward dip where her belly button would surely be. He imagined kissing that tender spot, the way she would arch her hips when he did, and he almost lost himself.

His hands continued upward so that his thumbs were cupped under each breast and his fingertips grazed the bare skin just above the neckline of her gown. Then he stroked his thumbs upward over her nipples. Daniela gasped. Even through her gown and shift, she could feel his touch. Her nipples rose to attention as he continued to stroke them, giving them the attention they demanded.

She broke their kiss as a long moan escaped her mouth. Eric watched her lean back, her creamy white throat and breasts exposed as she let the visceral intensity of the sensation wash over her. She was completely uninhibited and it made him want her even more.

Daniela seemed to realize he was watching her. She brought her face back down and met his eyes. He continued to move his hands across her breasts. She had to dig her fingernails into her palms to keep some sort of grip on reality.

"I ..." Daniela gulped, showing an uncharacteristic vulnerability. Eric froze, his fingers halfway curved over her breast, steeling himself in case she was about to ask him to stop. Instead, she said shyly: "I have never ... done this before."

He chuckled, a rich rumble from deep inside his broad chest. "Don't worry, I have."

"That worries me even more!" She exclaimed.

Eric wrapped his arms around her waist and pulled her tighter against him. He felt her melt into his arms, a sigh rippling through her body. Her breasts pushed against his chest and her hips leaned into his unconsciously.

He lowered his lips again to her neck. She tilted her head back, a shudder of anticipation shaking her body as his hot breath tickled her throat. He placed a trail of kisses from beneath her chin to the tender spot just below her ear. "Let me show you."

She inclined her head slightly so she could meet his eyes. His pale blue eyes caught her darker ones. She could see the swirling desire in those light blue orbs, like clouds moving quickly across a stormy sky. With unwavering sureness, she nodded her head. It was all the invitation Eric needed. He moved his hand up into the mass of her hair and then pulled her mouth up to meet his.

Chapter 20

If she was not ruined before she stepped over his threshold, she would be well and truly done for by the time this evening passed. That was the only coherent thought that entered Dani's head as Eric kissed her again. This time his hands were on her shoulders, stroking the delicate skin that peeked out from the top of the cap sleeves.

But she did not want to leave. She wanted to know what every sensation would feel like.

Daniela leaned into his kiss, offering her mouth and body freely. She curled her tongue around his, reaching in and touching the depths of his mouth just as she had felt him do with hers. And she finally allowed herself to touch him. For weeks, she had been imagining what his strong shoulders and chest would feel like beneath her hands. She need not imagine a moment more.

He was not wearing a waistcoat or tailcoat. He wore only a simple cream-colored linen shirt. There was a deep-v cut to his mid-chest, and then three buttons southward. Determined to finally see that broad chest she had been dreaming about, Daniela pulled her mouth from his. Eric looked temporarily confused. But she lifted her hands to the first button and he saw the look of concentration on her face.

She undid one button. Then the next. His chest was tanned – *how could it be tanned? Was the man spending time out of doors unclothed?* Beneath her fingertips, she could feel the curls of wiry hair on his chest. It undid her. She almost lost her nerve. Then she felt the tremor that raced through him as her fingertips grazed her bare chest. And she realized that she was having the same effect on him as he was on her. She fumbled with the last button but managed to get it open. Then she spread her hands over his chest greedily, amazed at the feeling of his muscles rippling beneath her fingertips.

Eric moaned. "For a novice, you have me entirely at your will," he said, his jaw clenched.

Daniela did not even have a moment to enjoy that victory. Eric took back control, sliding his hands around her waist, down her back, and cupping her bottom.

Behind them on the hearth, a log shifted, falling apart and setting a new round of flames afire.

Eric captured her mouth again as he lifted her up. Dani wrapped her legs around his waist instinctively. He carried her three steps to the sofa that stood before the roaring fire. He kneeled carefully, lowering her down onto the plush padded green damask, now a dark emerald in the firelight.

As she laid back on the sofa, she tilted her head back and offered him her mouth. But Eric did not take it. Instead, he leaned down and placed a kiss on the sensitive flesh just above the neckline of her gown. Then he kissed a line along the edge of her gown, peeling it down an extra inch with his fingers to slide his tongue over her tender bosom. It was the most exquisite torture. Daniela longed for him to touch her breasts more boldly, as he had before, but she was so caught up in the sensations of desire that she could hardly keep her head, let alone ask for what she wanted.

Then she felt Eric's hand at her ankle. He had touched her there before when giving her a leg up into the saddle. His hand slid up her calf, then back to her ankle, then up her calf again. She had foregone stockings. With the unseasonably warm spring weather, she had just gotten out of the habit of wearing them.

That meant that his fingers touched her bare skin. And if the feeling of his hands on her through her exercise rider breeches had been alluring, the feel of his strong fingers on her smooth skin was intoxicating.

But his hands did not stop there. While one hand moved up her leg the other lifted her skirts. At some point, he or she had removed her boots. She had no memory of it.

His fingers and his lips touched her inner thigh at the same time. It was like a bolt of lightning had struck her. She felt the tremor go through her entire body. No one had ever touched her there. When she washed her legs while bathing, or pulled a stocking up, she might touch that part of her legs. But another person, a man – it was completely overwhelming.

Eric seemed to sense the intensity of her emotions. He paused, his mouth an inch from her soft skin, his hands on her knees, and looked up at her awaiting a response. It was the first moment that Dani paused and wondered if she had gone too far over this precipice.

But she looked down into Eric's eyes, clear and honest and good, and she felt the peace and surety return. She breathed out slowly and nodded her head, her bottom lip caught between her teeth.

Eric took her signal with alacrity. He ran his tongue from the inside of her right knee, up her inner thigh to the juncture of her hips. He stopped just short of touching her most private place, letting his hand catch up. He used both hands to move the damp muslin skirts away so that her legs and hips were revealed. She had finely molded legs, muscled and strong from hours and days spent on horseback. He could easily imagine days and weeks spent getting to know their every curve. But tonight, now, he was focused on showing her the ultimate pleasure.

His fingers stroked rhythmically, tapping out a line of sensation along her thighs. Her skin glistened in the firelight. Although she did not know what it meant, he could see her desire flowing from her in a stream of wetness. He felt himself harden. But he was determined to give to her first; for a reason he could not name, it was essential that she find her satisfaction and ride those waves of ecstasy before he gave in to the pleasure he knew would be found in her sweet and supple body.

Daniela felt exposed and yet completely open. It was as if a new part of her had been introduced to the world. She had never imagined a feeling like this. Eric had opened her legs, expertly coaxing them apart with caresses and kisses. The most vulnerable part of her body was exposed and yet she felt completely at ease. In fact, eager.

Then his mouth touched her. He lowered his tongue to her most sensitive core and she thought she would expire on the spot.

His touch was feather-light at first. Eric breathed in and out, letting the hot air touch her, wash over her. Then he touched his lips to her lower ones – a line of kisses along the sweet, swollen lips until he reached her tender bud of pleasure. When he pressed his lips there her whole body shivered. But that wasn't enough. She did not know what was coming but he did. He knew that by the time he was done her hips would be bucking under his mouth. He hoped he would hear her cry out; those cries of desperation already echoing in his ears.

"Eric, Eric, Eric," she moaned. His name on her lips … he had heard it only a handful of times before. It was like music. Like a hymn sung by angels.

"Hold on, my sweet," he said softly. His hand slid up her leg, over her hip, and gripped her hand in his own. Their fingers intertwined. Then he flicked his finger over her hot little bud.

Dani cried out. She had never felt such intensity before. And then he did it again. And again. Her grip tightened on his hand. He could not look up but Eric was sure her joints were white with squeezing. She was holding on for dear life.

There was a crash from behind them. The fire was fully ablaze, lighting the entire room, filling it with heat, spilling long golden rays over their bodies.

Eric could not wait a moment longer. He closed his mouth on her body, flicking his tongue back and forth again and again. Dani raised her hips, pushing upwards against his mouth. Her fingernails dug into his hand, a continuous stream of unintelligible sounds escaping her beautiful lips.

She started to whimper. He could tell that she was close. "Hold on, my love," Eric murmured. He alternated between flicking his tongue back and forth over her hot button and kissing her warm folds, his tongue darting in and out of her deep center.

Dani did not know what was happening. But the feeling in her loins took complete control. She arched upwards. She heard herself speak but could not attribute the words.

"Please, please," she begged, though she did not even know what she was asking for.

But Eric did. He shifted his focus, keeping his tongue at her button of pleasure, moving his tongue back and forth, up and down, swirling around. The taste of her was intoxicating; more alluring than any liquor or aged wine. She arched her hips and then she froze. The sound that poured from her was primal. The wetness that poured over him was sweet and hot.

Eric held tight to her hand as she came down, her breath slowing over long minutes as she regulated and adjusted. He was as hard as he had ever been. But he held back, his eyes fixed upon her. He rested his chin upon her stomach, reveling in the rise and fall of her beautiful breasts and the quiver of her chin as she drew in a long steadying breath.

"I had no idea," she finally said.

A deep chuckle resonated from inside Eric's chest, reverberating against her body, pressed together as tightly as they were.

"You *have* no idea," he said huskily.

He pulled back and came to rest on his haunches. Daniela immediately felt the loss and reached for him. Eric gained his feet and then leaned down to the sofa and scooped her up into his arms. Hooking one arm behind her neck and the other behind her knees, he leaned down and kissed her thoroughly.

Daniela wrapped her arms around his neck and pulled him tightly to her, as if she could not possibly get him close enough. "Let me show you the rest," Eric breathed, his forehead pressed to hers.

"Please," she murmured back.

Eric climbed the steps to his bedroom two at a time, Dani ensconced tightly against his chest.

Chapter 21

Eric fumbled a bit with the door to his bedroom. He was not used to trying to open it while holding a beautiful woman in his arms. He felt a little flutter of embarrassment. But Dani seemed completely oblivious. She was gazing up at him with adoring eyes.

As they entered the room, her head turned to take in his private inner sanctum. She bit her lip to keep from giggling. "It definitely … has a masculine sensibility."

Eric looked around the room as she might have – the bed was neatly made with a striped navy-blue coverlet and two pillows. There were no plush blankets or decorative pillows. Aside from the bed, there was a dark mahogany dressing table that did double duty as a writing desk. A coat tree stood in the corner, with a few overcoats hanging ready. And that was it.

He flushed. "It has been a long time ... my mother died several years before my father. And since I inherited the title –"

"I don't need to know any more," Daniela said firmly. The last thing she wanted at this moment was to hear anything about his past romantic exploits. She did not think of him as a rake or a rogue and she wanted to keep that image intact in her mind. At least for tonight.

They awkwardly avoided each other's eyes. A difficult task considering that Eric still held her in his arms.

Daniela's stomach made a loud and demanding groan. She blushed, but Eric laughed aloud, his head back and his chest shaking. *Lord, he was so handsome when he smiled like that.* She could almost ignore her empty stomach. She so badly wanted to kiss those lips, stretched into that endearing smile.

Her stomach rumbled again.

Well, almost.

Eric chuckled again as he lowered Dani to her feet. "I guess you did not stop for supper while you were searching out lodgings?"

Dani smiled sheepishly. "I was a bit too preoccupied," she admitted.

He looked toward the door, which still stood ajar. "I have dismissed the staff for the evening, but I suppose I could go try and rustle something up ..." he trailed off dubiously.

"Simple is fine. Bread, cheese, fruit?" She suggested.

Eric nodded, rubbing his hand across his chin as he considered. "Alright. I will go down to the kitchen and see what I can find. Make yourself comfortable." He glanced around the room and shook his head as he chuckled again. "As comfortable as you can."

The smile glowed on her face long after Eric had left. Daniela stood in the middle of the room, her arms wrapped around herself, feeling the warmth permeate her body. As if he had lit some internal candle that could not be doused.

The rain outside still pounded down steady and strong. The morning, the race … seemed a lifetime away. Daniela felt like she had been through a catharsis of sorts; like the rain had washed away her inhibitions and her worries, leaving behind clarity about her desire and her needs. And what she wanted was Eric.

She'd had time to think while she was turned away from inn after tavern after boardinghouse that afternoon and into the evening. Eric had told her aunt quite clearly that he did not wish to marry her. It had stung so much more deeply than she had expected. Marriage had never entered Daniela's mind until her aunt threw those words out into the universe, knowing they would cause pain.

Daniela had always considered herself proud. If she'd read her own story in a book, she would have cheered the heroine right out of town onto the muddy road, cold and alone but fiercely independent. But once the cold rain had stripped away all of her edifices she found that what her heart wanted was all too clear. Even if there was no marriage, there could still be tonight. If she was ruined, she might as well have what the world would think she had. If society was determined to throw her and Eric together, then why should she fight it? Why should she hold back from something – someone – that she wanted so desperately?

She could ignore the questions of the morning for the promise of a night spent in his arms.

He returned less than ten minutes later with a tray laden with food: a half-loaf of bread, cheese wrapped in waxed paper, a couple of pears, and a bottle of wine.

Eric looked curiously at the setup Dani had made. She'd gone through one of the mysterious doors that opened off of the bedroom and found a small closet with an armoire. On the bed, she had spread out a sheet that she'd found. A servant had banked the fire before retiring for the night; Dani was able to stoke it back to life with little effort and use the flame to light several candles.

"I thought we'd have a bit of a picnic." Dani nodded towards the bed. Eric took her hint and laid out his tray of offerings on top of the white sheet she'd put over the coverlet.

Dani climbed onto the bed, pulling her skirts up over her knees so she could sit cross-legged, revealing her calves and hinting at the sweetness at the center of her body.

"This is already the best picnic I've ever had," Eric said bluntly.

She grabbed one of the pears and took a bite. "I'd better be quick. You look like —"

"I'd like to devour you instead of the food?"

His light blue eyes had gone as dark and stormy as sapphires. Dani swallowed hard.

"Precisely."

"Then let's eat, while I still have some modicum of self-control." Eric lowered himself down to the bed, sitting beside her but not close enough to touch. He'd tasted the depths of her sweetness, but he had yet to fully join with her. And he was fairly throbbing with anticipation.

Dani took another bite of her pear. He watched as her lips curved around the tender green skin, her straight white teeth biting into the tender flesh, her mouth sucking at the juices to keep them from escaping. He forced himself to focus on opening the bottle of wine.

"You said you told your aunt and uncle you were headed for home. To Gainsborough?" He asked, desperate for a distraction.

She nodded, licking up a bit of pear juice that had dripped down the side of her hand to her wrist. Eric felt his groin tighten.

"Yes, I had every intention of hiring a carriage to take me to Gainsborough right away. But it did not take long for me to realize that every conveyance for twenty miles is staying put in Cambridge or Newmarket until the end of the racing meet."

"So, you decided to stay."

"I don't think I really wanted to go, to be honest." She sighed as she took a bite of the bread. A look of satisfaction drifted over her face as she slowly chewed.

"I do want to go home," she clarified between bites. "There is no way I will be returning to my aunt and uncle. But Mercury is special."

"Yes, he is." *Not half as special as you.* Eric finally managed to pop open the bottle of wine. He looked at the tray he'd brought upstairs. "I seem to have forgotten the glasses."

With a mischievous gleam in her eye, Dani leaned forward and held out her hand. He handed her the bottle willingly. Without pausing, she lifted the slender neck to her lips and took a long drink. When she lowered the bottle, her lips were stained with dark red wine.

She smiled at him coyly, then offered him back the bottle. Eric closed his eyes and drank deeply. Maybe the alcohol would dull his senses a little. Sitting here across the bed from her, he could hardly keep his mind on the food. Her body's noisy declaration of the need for nourishment was the only thing keeping him in check.

He cleared his throat. "I thought your father was in Ireland."

A faraway look came over her dark eyes. "I hope that he is home by now."

Eric felt himself calm fractionally. "Will his business have been resolved so quickly?"

"I don't know. When the Irish lord first sent his letter to my father making his accusations, we thought it was some kind of jest. It seemed so absurd. Then his man of business appeared and *his* demands were more persistent."

"What did he want?"

"Well, they wanted a refund for what they'd paid for the colt, to start with. When my father refused, saying that their accusations were false, the requests became more dire."

Eric quirked an eyebrow.

"They threatened to go public with their knowledge – to report it to contacts within the Jockey Club." Dani fiddled with the piece of bread in her hands, ripping it into smaller and smaller pieces as she spoke.

"The Jockey Club will not take such an accusation lightly. It will have to be investigated," Eric said.

Dani nodded sadly. "My father has spent the last three decades of his life building the farm. He started with nothing; a second son, a soldier. And now –"

"Now he is one of the most respected names in British horseracing," Eric finished for her. He saw the pride on her face at his words. And the pain as it faltered.

"But for how much longer?" She asked gloomily.

"So, he went to Ireland to try and make good with the lord who made the accusations in the first place?"

"He hoped that by speaking directly to his lordship, rather than through agents, they would be able to come to terms. I know that he's been advised to pay the man off. And he certainly could. The stud farm is extremely profitable. But his pride … I don't think it will allow him such a measure." Not sure what else to say, Dani took a bite of cheese just to give herself something to do.

Eric touched her hand gently. Slowly, she raised her eyes from the spot on the coverlet she had been staring at. His hand reached over and he stroked his thumb down her face. He didn't need to tell her how sorry he was for her; those emotive eyes said it all. And when he leaned forward and kissed her, it was an offer of comfort and closeness that said – *at least today, at least right now, you are not alone.*

Chapter 22

The kiss started soft and sweet.

Eric was offering comfort and warmth. His tongue moved tentatively into her mouth, his movements slow as he drew her tongue into an undulating dance. His thumb stroked up and down her cheek again and again. He felt her relax into him, her body melting into his.

He was such a good kisser. At least in her inexperienced estimation. The way he moved his lips against hers, creating friction intermixed with softness … how he timed the stroke of his hands with the movement of his tongue into her mouth … the effect was intoxicating. Much more so than the bottle of wine they had shared.

Dani felt herself deepening their embrace. After what he had done to her downstairs, how he had made her quiver and cry out in exaltation … there was no going back. She allowed herself to begin exploring his body. She'd been imagining what it would feel like to have those taut muscles beneath her hands. Now she slid her hands inside his shirt and gripped his arms tightly.

Eric responded in kind, sliding his hands up and down her arms then over her shoulders and along her collarbone. His fingers deftly unlaced the top few rungs of her gown so that it loosened and fell down her shoulders, exposing more skin to his touch. He kissed his way along her chin, down her neck, along her collarbone, and out to her shoulder. He paused for a second. Freckles. They were faint, but when the firelight hit her just so, they glowed a chestnut brown against her otherwise pale skin. He promised himself he would endeavor to kiss every single one before the night was through.

Dani leaned back and braced herself against the bed, nearly upending the tray of food and drink still laid out there. Before the laugh had time to bubble out of her, Eric had grabbed the tray and moved it adroitly to the floor. Then he returned to her, burying his mouth in her neck.

She wanted to touch him the way he had touched her. Very deliberatively she slid her hands down from where they held his shoulders, over his back, and around to his hips. He was kissing her neck. *Thank god.* She needed her mouth free to take the deep breath that would give her the courage to make good on her most wanton impulses.

She moved her hands to the ties of his breeches. He stiffened immediately. Dani almost withdrew her hands, but then she heard the slow release of air as he breathed out through his teeth. Her capable hands, usually at work on horse bridles or her stays, efficiently unfastened his breeches. She started to pull them down his hips. Eric slid off the bed, breaking the contact between them. He hooked his thumbs inside the waistline and looked at her meaningfully. She nodded her head almost imperceptibly. He slid the garment to the floor.

His heart was hammering in his chest. Eric watched for her reaction. Would she be scared or offput? He knew beyond a doubt that she was a virgin. She'd certainly never seen a man like this before. But when he looked into her eyes they were steady. More than steady – they were gleaming with unbridled desire.

Dani moved so she was sitting on the edge of the bed. Her garments were loose around her shoulders where Eric had been exploring with his hands and mouth. Her hair was coming down over her shoulders, red-gold flames whose tips pointed downward to the fire beneath.

With the same boldness that had allowed her to sit atop an invaluable thoroughbred in the guise of man, she reached out and took him in her hand. Eric thought her touch alone was enough to push him over the edge. Her palm was at once hot and cool. Her small hands wrapped around his rigid length rocked him intensely. Then she began to move her hands slowly up and down, showing him the same tender regard he had given to her.

Eric's head fell back and a primal, guttural sound emerged from his throat. The friction of the callouses on her palms from hours spent in the saddle, against the smoothness of his skin, the tentative gentleness contrasted with the determination to please him … it

One Race to Ruin

was too much. He was going to lose himself on the spot.

He reached down and grabbed her hands, pulling her up to stand and fixing his mouth on hers. Now he kissed her ferociously, as if he might somehow be able to actually devour her sweet flesh.

Dani broke away, her gaze worried. "Did I … I'm sorry. Did I do something wrong?"

Eric answered her with another smothering kiss. When they came back up for air she looked somewhat mollified. But the question still sat in her eyes.

"No. You did everything right. *Too* right."

She blushed epically, the pink rising from her rounded areolas to the tops of her delicately arched eyebrows. His gaze drawn downward, Eric planted a kiss on her cheek as he murmured: "Now it's my turn."

He worshipped her breasts. He cupped them in each of his hands, the curve of his palms mirroring the curve of the rounded fullness. She took a deep breath, her entire chest heaving up and down, her breasts moving against his palms. Mesmerized, he moved his thumbs in unison, flicking them upwards over her hardened pink nipples. Dani let out a sharp little gasp. But Eric couldn't drag his eyes away. He leaned forward and drew a circle around one nipple with his tongue, marveling at the ripples of gooseflesh that rose across her pale skin. Then he moved his mouth to the other breast and repeated the act.

Dani had never known such a feeling existed. She'd bound her breasts every day for weeks to avoid detection. When she returned home and undid her wrappings she'd felt intense relief and satisfaction. But beyond that, she had never felt any particular sensations around her breasts. She knew men were fascinated with them – now she knew why. Honestly, she did not think she'd ever look at a woman's breasts the same way again. Not that she was doing much thinking at that moment.

She had crossed into the realm of physical sensation, where thoughts came as hot and fast and incoherently as if she were intoxicated. Every time a thought occurred to her a new sensation flooded her senses, making it impossible to focus or think. The one persistent thought that kept pushing to the surface was excruciatingly simple: *Eric, Eric, Eric.*

Eric had known women. He'd been a young university lad – though much more circumspect than the young men who had bothered Daniela in the Cambridge square. And once he had come of age and come to London as the future Earl of Fordham, he'd enjoyed his fair share of bawdy houses and even a handful of *ton* widows.

But he had never felt this kind of connection to any of them. He'd considered himself an attentive lover. It only seemed fair. Pleasure was a two-sided coin. But it had always felt a bit like a duty. With Dani, he was so focused on making her feel and enjoy all of the pleasures of love-making he could almost forget his own needs. *Almost.*

Her caresses were becoming bolder. Although she was not holding his manhood in her hands any longer, she was moving her hips rhythmically against him, reaching instinctively for joining. Eric could not hold back much longer. As his mouth moved between her breasts and down toward her navel, he finished unfastening her gown and slid it off of her. What remained of her undergarments quickly followed. Finally, she was fully naked before him.

His breath caught in his throat. The cool gray and blue of the coverlet made a striking contrast to her pale skin, bathed in gold by the firelight. Her hair glowed around her face and shoulders like a candle. Like a flame, drawing him in.

Dani couldn't wait either. She reached up, put her hands on his shoulders, and drew him down to her. Eric put one knee down between her legs, spreading them easily. Her hand slid down from his shoulder to his hip, guiding him forward as if she was afraid he might change his mind. He could not have stopped now if he tried.

Knowing it was her first time, he leaned forward and kissed her, moving his tongue into her mouth at the same time that his quivering cock entered her warm folds. He hoped to distract her from any pain or discomfort.

Dani felt an uncomfortable pinch followed by the most singular sensation – of being filled, completed, whole. She heard Eric groan. Dani opened her eyes to watch his face. His shiny black brows were knitted together in a look of intense concentration. His lips pursed as his breath came hot and fast. He wasn't looking at her now. His luminous blue eyes had flitted half-closed as he too was carried away on waves of passion.

Just as before, when they were downstairs before the fire and his mouth had done those magical things to her, Dani felt the intensity of building toward something. This time she knew what to expect, but it came over her much faster than before.

All of a sudden, she was climaxing, her hips bucking against him and crying out with completely uncontrolled wantonness. Eric had concentrated so hard on holding himself back. When she lost control of herself and gave in entirely to her pleasure he had no choice but to follow her. Two strokes, another, and then he was exploding inside of her. He heard the sound that came from deep inside his chest, a rumble that turned into something resembling a roar. Daniela matched it with her ferocious cry of pleasure.

They fell back onto the bed together, his body covering hers. Afraid of hurting her with his solid frame on her more petite one, Eric rolled onto the bed beside her. Dani made a little mewling sound of loss as he pulled out and away. Reacting without thought, he slid his arm underneath her shoulder and rolled her towards him, cradling her head in the hollow of his shoulder. Daniela curved her leg around his so that their bodies were fit closer together.

The last thing either of them remembered as they drifted off to sleep was Eric turning his head and pressing a kiss into her soft, slightly damp hair, and deep sighs of satisfaction flowing through them both.

Chapter 23

As the early morning rays of light started to filter in, Eric felt the carefree pleasure of the night before start to ebb away. Dani still slept soundly. He was able to slide from the bed and sit upon the edge, his profile carved like a statue in the golden morning light.

The side of his body that was illuminated faced the window, where he could see horses already being turned out into the pasture. He knew that only a few miles away the stables at Newmarket were already abuzz with activity. Exercise riders would be taking horses along the training gallops. Grooms would be brushing out their shiny coats. Stable boys would deliver the morning feed to the horses – fresh hay and grain to those horses that would not run today, a more calculated offering for those who would be on the track in just a few hours' time vying for the finish line.

The rain had cleared. Although the sun was shining brightly now and there were just a few scant clouds high in the sky, the turf would be wet and sloppy for all of today's races. By the time the 2000 Guineas was run the track would be heavily churned up by all of the previous races. These were the kind of racing conditions that universally made trainers, jockeys, and riders' insides churn with unease.

Taylor had staff patrolling the Earl of Fordham's stable block throughout the night to ensure no further tampering. At post time Mercury would emerge onto the track and have his run at the title. Eric had prayed for months now that he would have enough to finish the job.

But none of that was what caused the deep furrow in Eric's brow.

The other half of his face was in shadow. He gazed down at Dani, her body twined in the sheets and her freckled shoulder peeking out. She had rolled away from him in the night so that when he awoke his body was curved around hers in a snug s-shape. Just the curve of her shoulder made his body start to yearn for her again.

But it could not happen again.

He was the Earl of Fordham. And yes, he was expected to marry a woman of status, to find a countess who would bear heirs and complement him. But that woman could not be Dani.

The reaction he had when her aunt asked him – it had been immediate and visceral. Not because he did not desire her, but because he could not fathom that path. Could not think about bringing another person into the mess that had become his life. Least of all Dani, the first and only woman who had ever inspired anything in him beyond the physical. The nearly twelve months since his father's passing had been the worst of his life. Wrought with worry and anxiety. Eric would not have wished such an existence on an enemy – *with Bradford Kenner, perhaps, being the exception.*

Last night, when she had finally unloaded the depth of her fears surrounding the situation with her father, the time and energy it would take to help rebuild what had been lost ... that was when he had truly known. She would give herself to that pursuit with every breath she took. She had to. And he would not ask her to do otherwise.

Then there was the accident itself. Eric had been mulling it over ever since his conversation in the stable yard with Taylor and the head groom. It did not much matter whether Kenner or the mystery brute were to blame. Dani's association with him had put her in danger and that was not a situation he could allow to continue. He was at a loss for how to salvage her reputation but he'd be damned if he would allow the perfect angel of a woman to pay for his mistakes with her life.

More than anything he wished that he could step up and save her – offer her the financial resources and social clout with which to rebuild her family's reputation and save her own. But he was barely keeping his own estate together. And even if they won the 2000 Guineas today, it would be a long and arduous slog to rebuild the earldom's lost fortunes. It would be a start, certainly. But he could not ask it of her.

If they had met in five years, maybe it could have been different ...

Another thought wormed its way into his consciousness. There was a way.

His eyes traveled to the corner of the room, where two of his overcoats were hung on a coat tree: one gray and one brown. In the left pocket of the gray coat was a piece of paper. A piece of paper with a number upon it. A number that when he had first seen it, had seemed preposterous for what it implied.

But a new thought occurred to him ... what it could mean now. Not the salvation or reconstruction of his estate and fortune but the freedom to choose. Freedom to build a life with Daniela. The only woman who had ever mattered. And, he was beginning to realize, the only woman who ever would.

Would she ever forgive him? Must he tell her? If he did, she would surely feel betrayed. She had given her heart and soul to Mercury and him, just as he had her. If he did not tell her, she would wonder at the source of the funds that resolved the grievous state of his affairs overnight. He might be able to convince her of some miracle – an unexpected inheritance, a generous investor ... he turned over the possibilities in his head over and over again. The image of Daniela in his life, in his bed, not just now but forevermore – it was so tempting. His body started to tingle with anticipation. His heart ... pulsed in a way he could never have imagined. No matter what he decided, she had crawled into his heart and would not move. He would carry her with him always.

But the cost. It crept back into his consciousness, dousing the warmth that had lit inside of him like a bucket of cold water on a campfire.

Cheating ... would he ever be able to forgive himself?

One Race to Ruin

Eric shook himself. The action shook the whole bed. But still, Daniela did not stir from her slumber. Rather, a little smile of contentment turned up the corners of her soft pink lips.

He could not think about what could have been or might have been because it could not be. If he was half the man he thought himself, he would see Daniela home safely today and then he would bid her a final adieu.

She rolled over in her sleep, stretching her arms above her head and lifting her breasts above the sheet.

Perhaps it could happen one more time.

Chapter 24

"I can call for a maid if you'd like, to help with your ..." He trailed off blankly, having no idea what Daniela might want. For all his encounters with women, he had never had a mistress or ongoing romantic relationship. There had never been a lady whom he had cared for enough to wonder. Most of the women he had known departed in the dark of night.

"And further scandalize your staff?" Daniela said, laying her garments out on the bed. They were terribly wrinkled from a night spent on the floor of his bedroom stuffed inside her shoulder bag.

"Short of sneaking you out the back door, I think some visibility is inevitable." He hoped she did not want to sneak away as inconspicuously as possible. Though it would clearly have been the smarter choice, he was loath to part with her yet. He trusted his staff to keep their secrets. They had kept his father's financial milieu quiet for years.

"I am quite good at sneaking," she said with a twinkle in her eye. "But I do see your point." She tapped her finger to her lip, considering her options. The action mesmerized him. Eric caught the finger before she brought it down another time. He pressed the fingertip to his own lips, then sucked it into his mouth. He felt the shiver that pulsed through her body.

"We ought to leave soon," she breathed as he lowered his lips to hers. But that was no real protest. She welcomed his kiss, opening her mouth and inviting his tongue into her warm depths. She could easily forget about Newmarket, the race, her creased clothing …

"You're right. Mercury will be calmer for Greene if he sees you this morning." Eric chuckled at the look of disappointment on her face. "I can arrange for a carriage to take you into Newmarket and then I can ride in separately to avoid any scandal."

Dani laughed aloud. When she saw the seriousness of Eric's expression she sobered a bit. "I have come this far already. I would like to go to the race together." Her voice was quiet but very serious.

Eric felt an emotion swelling inside of him that he dared not name. For if he did he feared he would never be able to walk away from her. "Alright," he managed to say hoarsely.

Daniela rewarded him with a smile, the sprinkle of barely-there freckles across her cheeks rising with the corners of her mouth.

"I suppose I'm already ruined. I would rather not arrive at Newmarket a disheveled mess and give the masses more cause for disdain. Call the maid."

Eric's maid had been skittish but sufficient. As a maid in a bachelor's household, she was not used to attending to a lady. Her day mostly consisted of changing sheets, cleaning rooms, and bringing up tea. And of course, being asked to wait upon the woman who had spent the night in the unmarried earl's bedroom was enough to shake even the steadiest of servants.

Daniela was torn between her embarrassment, desire to insist that she was not one of *those* women, and the persistent confidence in the merit of her own choices. *She* had chosen to come to Eric's house, and his bed, the night before. And she did not have any regrets. To spare them both awkwardness, she asked the maid to see about steaming the wrinkles out of her garments. That kept the young woman busy for almost an hour, giving Daniela enough time to clean herself quickly using the basin of warm water the maid had arrived with, dress in her underthings, and brush her hair.

By the time the maid returned Dani was seated in front of the mirror at the dressing table, attempting to arrange her hair.

"Oh, you have worked a miracle!" Daniela exclaimed when she saw the dress and jacket draped neatly over the maid's arm.

The woman allowed herself the smallest of smiles. Daniela decided to press her luck.

"Perhaps you would be amenable to trying to manage one more?" She held up her hairbrush in one hand and a pile of hairpins in the other. While Dani was quite adept at piling and pinning her hair beneath a man's cap, achieving an elegant chignon was another matter entirely.

The maid could hardly refuse such a direct request. But she also did not look entirely opposed. She carefully hung the dress she had meticulously steamed and then took the hairbrush from Daniela.

The first few strokes were slow and cautious. But as the maid grew more comfortable her movements became more confident. Daniela let out a little moan of enjoyment. It was always a treat to have one's hair brushed.

"You have lovely hair, Miss …"

"Miss Rames," Daniela supplied.

"Miss Rames. It is such a fine color." The maid separated it into sections, starting to work the unruly curls into a style.

"Thank you. It's a bit stubborn," Daniela giggled as the other woman lost track of a curl and made a little mewl of frustration. "Look at that! Two miracles in one morning!" Daniela cried a few minutes later, turning her head this way and that in front of the mirror to examine the intricate work the young woman had done.

"Talking about me?" Eric said from the doorway.

Daniela gave him a pert little smile. "Hardly. I was complimenting this young woman's work."

"Indeed." His voice was gravelly, his gaze appreciative as it raked over her sitting there in her underclothes. Daniela felt the heat rising in her chest; she was sure if she glanced down, she would see the blush rising over her breasts. She felt the maid tense beside her.

Daniela forced herself to look away from Eric's stormy blue eyes and back to the young woman. "Thank you for your help. I won't monopolize your time any longer."

The maid curtsied and retreated quickly, clearly ill-at-ease with the situation. It was a sharp reminder to Daniela that while things might feel easy within the safe confines of Eric's home, the outside world awaited them.

Despite his offer of a carriage to take them to Newmarket, Dani insisted on riding. She had correctly observed that the carriage would do little but delay the inevitable stir that they would cause. And they were both more comfortable on horseback.

It never crossed his mind to ask her to distance herself from him. This melee was as much his fault as hers. More, he felt, because he had understood the consequences more thoroughly than she had. And because he had less to lose from the unraveling of their masquerade. As the Earl of Fordham and a man, certain things would always be forgiven. The world was not so kind to an untitled young woman whose family reputation was already about to come into question.

One Race to Ruin

They rode into Newmarket side by side. At first, Eric thought that perhaps the extent of the scandal was overblown. The town was very busy and no one paid them much attention. They were just two more among a huge throng of high society attendees at the biggest race of the spring meeting.

The first indication that he was wrong came just on the edge of town as they were leaving the village to ride towards the racecourse. Two well-dressed, middle-aged women stood chatting outside of the nicest inn the town had to offer, waiting for their carriage to be brought around. When they spotted Daniela and Eric they fell silent and stared openly.

Eric looked over at her quickly, but she kept her eyes trained forward. Dani showed no indication that she had seen the woman or regarded them at all. He felt something new start to grow in his chest – he thought it might be pride.

But that was not the worst of it, not by far. On a racing day, the racecourse was teeming with people. On the day of the 2000 Guineas there was hardly room to breathe. Some were dropped off in carriages that would return later. If the attendees owned horses or knew someone willing to share stable or paddock space, they might ride in as Eric and Daniela were doing. But the vast majority of patrons elected to walk the one-and-a-half-mile distance from the village to the racecourse.

And mounted as they were above the throng, Dani and Eric drew all the eyes.

Dani had known there would be attention and that it certainly would not be positive. But she had not realized how widely the scandal had spread. She might have been imagining it, but it felt like the eyes of every other person – regardless of class or gender – were on her. Her aunt and uncle would be here somewhere. The proper thing to do would be to go and find them, apologize, and then slink away into the ruinous shame that society seemed to think she deserved.

Well, she was having none of that. She was the daughter of Nathaniel Rames, the most well-known and well-respected racehorse breeder in Britain. She rode better than most of the exercise riders, jockeys, and certainly horse-mad *haute ton* members in attendance today. And she was the exercise rider for the magnificent horse that was about to win the 2000 Guineas. She held her head high and rode past her detractors without even the slightest hint of acknowledgment.

Dani felt her heart twinge at the thought of her father. She would see him soon enough no matter the outcome of the race. Would he be disappointed in her? She did not think so. When the news of her ruin reached him – whether it be by her own letter or some other means – she felt certain of his love and support. So long as this nonsense with the Irish lord had been resolved, she felt confident her scandal would not impact her father's business. A ruined daughter would mean little to the horseracing-obsessed lords of English nobility. Whereas a breeder whose reputation could not be trusted or who faced condemnation from the Jockey Club would be devastating.

Eric did not think Dani could surprise him, not after the events of the last twelve hours. And still, the way she maintained her composure and rode elegantly through the crowd – literally and figuratively above it all – his feelings for her deepened even more. Feelings he did not even dare to begin to examine.

They rode past the training grounds and crowds that were already beginning to jostle for good viewing positions for the day's races, towards the Earl of Fordham's stable block. They were greeted by Taylor and Greene, who were waiting for them looking rather anxious.

"What's wrong?" Eric dismounted immediately, handing his horse's reins over to a waiting stable hand. "Has something happened to Mercury?"

Taylor shook his head. "The beast is fit and fine. Ready to go. Not sure about the state of this ground. It will be a torn-up mess by the time the 2000 Guineas runs." He lifted his foot from the ground in demonstration, his boot making a loud sucking sound as it pulled away from the mud.

"We knew ye were coming. Spread like wildfire that the two of you were seen riding in from Cambridge together." Greene broke in, knowing that Eric was still waiting for an explanation. "The things we were hearing … they weren't exactly complimentary to Miss Rames." He spoke quietly but Daniela heard him clearly enough.

She climbed down from her horse without waiting for an assist. "I shall go and say good morning to Mercury, I think."

Eric watched her go, a deep frown on his face. "She's handling it extraordinarily well."

"Aye, well, she's a rare young woman." Greene agreed. "Her father will hear about this soon, there's no avoiding that. What will you do then?"

Surprised at the jockey's directness, Eric felt a deep clench of regret in his chest. "I don't know," he answered honestly. "I do not have much to offer a young woman at the moment."

Greene looked sorry for him, which made Eric feel worse. The older man clapped him on the shoulder sympathetically.

"Let's win this one today and then take the measure of things."

Satisfied that Dani and Eric were well enough, Taylor and Greene drifted away to continue talking strategy for the mucky race. How would it affect Mercury? Or the other entrants? Should they change the strategy they had decided on earlier in the week?

Alone for the first time all day, Eric walked to the edge of the paddock that adjoined the stable block. He leaned forward against the railing, staring absently at the horses that were there. They would not be racing today, so they got to enjoy their fill of the green pasture grass.

Then at the corner of his peripheral vision something caught his eye. Two shapes moving slowly, taking a circuitous route around the paddock and stable yard. No one would have known they had any intention other than two attendees hoping to get an up-close peek of the day's racing entrants. But the sight of them made a hard rock drop into the pit of Eric's stomach.

The tweed-man, no longer dressed in tweed but a dark gray suit with a bright red flourish in his breast pocket. His hulking companion was beside him, attired more simply but hardly inconspicuous given his size. They did not linger or even change pace. The smaller of the two tipped his hat to Eric as they continued to stroll along the opposite side of the paddock and then back towards the racecourse.

Greene had asked him what he was going to do. Watching the ridicule Dani had faced as they rode in, knowing that it would not go away ... likely it would haunt her forever, even if she did eventually manage to marry ...

Damnation, how had things gotten so complicated? All he wanted was to protect her, but neither choice would do it. If he did the selfish thing – married her and kept her at his side – he had not doubt that the passion and emotional connection they shared would grow into something even more beautiful. But not only would he be dooming Dani to a life of worry, an existence predicated on the success of the next race, he would be exposing her to danger. Those two men at the paddock had made things very clear – they were not going away.

Even if Mercury won today, there was still the Derby and the St. Ledger. Two more opportunities for the faceless villain and his stooges to put pressure and threaten Eric and anyone close to him.

Daniela spent the majority of the day in the stables with Mercury. She told herself she was not interested in the earlier races, that she needed to give Mercury her full attention so that he would have his best chance of winning. But in truth, she did not want to face the sneers and furtive glances of the other patrons. It had taken everything she had to ride through the crowd the first time.

Last night, she had only been able to think about what the evening would bring. This morning, she had shifted her focus to getting through the 2000 Guineas. She could not seem to plan her next move beyond that, whatever it may be.

Even though she was fashionably dressed – attending the races was, after all, a social event for the *ton* – she groomed Mercury herself. She combed out his long mane and tail. She brushed him again and again until his chestnut coat gleamed with every ray of sunshine that filtered down through the hayloft. She even lifted each of his hooves and inspected them thoroughly. She did not want there to be any physical reason he did not race to victory.

So focused was she on his grooming, Dani nearly jumped out of her skin when Eric appeared at the stall door.

"It's time to get him saddled."

Luckily, Mercury was still relaxed from his pampering and did not react to her skittishness.

"Alright. I suppose I will leave him to the groom," she sighed. Eric offered her his arm.

He led her down the aisle of the stable and out into the yard. It had clouded over somewhat since the bright sunshine of the morning. Eric followed her skyward glance. "I don't think it is going to rain again."

"I hope not," Dani said emphatically. She looked up at the sky for a long moment but seemed to agree that the prospects of a dry race looked promising. "He will handle well. The ground is churned up, it's true. But it will not change a horse as obstinate as him. He wants to win."

"You can tell that just from looking at him, can you?" Eric's eyes twinkled affectionately as he looked down at her.

"More than just looking at him. Don't forget, I have spent the last month on his back every single day …" she trailed off as they started to enter the more crowded parts of the track. "They certainly won't let me forget."

Eric tightened his grip on her arm. "Focus on Mercury. He is all that matters just now."

Dani nodded, swallowing her discomfort. She could not have agreed more.

They walked to the paddock where the horses were being assembled. Trainers, owners, and jockeys had already begun to assemble inside the central oval, although the horses were still *en route* from their respective stable blocks. As they approached the gate Dani released Eric's arm and stepped back. He turned back to her abruptly, his eyes questioning.

Her eyes were downcast. "This is your moment. I do not want to taint it with my …. scandal."

There were onlookers everywhere. This was the 2000 Guineas, after all. There were hundreds of people vying for a good spot to view the entrants as they began to arrive in the paddock. Despite that, Eric took her hand and replaced it firmly in his arm.

"This is your moment as much as mine. I would not be standing here without everything you have done."

Dani flushed, as she always did. But this time she did not mind. The compliment rushed through her, from the tops of her red-gold eyebrows to the tips of her toes beneath her stockings and boots. She accepted his arm and walked with him to join Taylor and Greene where they waited inside the paddock.

Mercury was ready. He entered the paddock frisky on his feet, nudging his head at his groom and prancing around energetically. To others, he might look unsettled. But to Dani and Eric, he was a pistol cocked and ready to fire. All they had to do was get him to the starting line.

They watched as he walked around the oval twice. On the third pass, the jockeys would mount. Eric and Taylor had already discussed it; the Earl of Fordham would give Greene his leg up, as his father had set the custom of doing before him. Dani and Taylor stepped back as Eric and Greene stepped closer to the edge of the oval. The groom leading Mercury was rounding the curve.

For just a moment, Eric and the jockey were alone. This was the moment, Eric realized in a flash. If he was going to amend the jockey's instructions or tell him to hold Mercury back ... this was his last chance. Eric could not see the two men sent by the fixer, but he knew they must be lurking somewhere nearby. They had certainly maintained a presence at the edge of his mind. Mercury was just moments away. Eric would need to step forward and offer his hands to lift Greene into the saddle.

With the mere seconds that remained, Eric looked back over his shoulder at Daniela Rames. She was standing beside Taylor, glowing like a candle. She belonged here, in this world of racing, and his life. But he could not give it to her unless he took the tweedman up on his offer. Eric was leaning forward, his mouth open to speak to Greene. Then Dani grabbed Taylor's arm in excitement, her eyes fixed on

One Race to Ruin

Mercury. He could see the confidence in her eyes, the way she glowed as she watched the horse she had worked with and loved so dearly.

Eric bit his lip hard. Mercury was there. He gave Greene a leg up and then they were off into the post parade.

There was no going back now.

Chapter 25

They found their spot on the rail quickly. Perfectly chosen just before the finish line. Eric could have watched from the stands; many owners were. It was a better view of the Rowley Mile, which was a long, expansive turf track. Here he would not know exactly what was happening until the horses came close enough to see. But most importantly, he would have a front-row seat to see the winner cross the finish line.

At his side, Dani gripped his arm tightly. She was watching the post parade, as the horses trotted from the paddock onto the track, with their pony riders in tow. Dani scanned the other horses with an assessing eye but her gaze kept going back to Mercury.

On his other side, Taylor had taken out his pipe and was puffing out rings of white smoke in rapid succession, completely oblivious to all of the other patrons crowded around them to watch the race.

As Eric looked from Dani to Taylor, he spotted another familiar figure standing at the rail a few yards away from them. His lip curled up in involuntary disdain when he laid eyes on Bradford Kenner.

He had no way of being sure whether it was Kenner or the fixers who had meddled with Dani's saddle. It was equally unclear if the stunt had been meant to reveal her identity or to do serious damage to Mercury's regular rider and therefore jeopardize his chances at winning the 2000 Guineas. But the uncertainty did not matter. Eric held Kenner responsible nonetheless.

Kenner was talking to a blonde-haired man who stood between him and his wife, Elizabeth. When he started to turn his head in their direction, Eric turned sharply to avoid meeting his gaze. The last thing he wanted at this moment was to exchange looks, let alone *words*, with the likes of Kenner.

Dani was caught off balance by his sudden movement. She turned her face up to his, searching for some hint to his discomfiture. But Eric had now turned his gaze back towards the starting line where the horses were trotting off to be lined up in their post positions.

She leaned into his solid frame. Crushed together as they were with all the other spectators down at the rail, no one noticed how closely they were standing or the continuous caresses that their hands laid upon each other.

As she looked out over the crowd behind them, Dani even allowed herself to lay her cheek against Eric's chest. She breathed in deeply, savoring his masculine scent – the whiff of his aftershave from his morning grooming routine, the smell of fresh hay and wet turf from the time spent on horseback and in the stables throughout the day. Her eyes were fluttering closed when a bright color caught her eye.

The color was so distinctive – a bright yellow hue favored by just one person that Daniela knew. Sure enough, as she squinted her eyes to get a better look, she was able to make out Winnie and her parents. Aunt Millie was dressed in dark burgundy, looking particularly conservative this afternoon. Daniela wasn't immediately able to tell if they had spotted her. Then she saw Winnie lift her left hand in greeting.

Either her aunt and uncle did not see her or they were choosing to ignore her existence. Both possibilities were fine with Daniela. She lifted her free hand and returned Winnie's greeting.

It was only fitting that her family was here to witness this race. It was for this horse, this race, and this man that she had supposedly sacrificed her future. Let them look on as Mercury rode to victory before hundreds – *nee thousands*! – of spectators. After today, she could never see them again and that would be just fine with her. Well, perhaps that was a bit harsh. She would happily see Winnie anytime and often.

Further thought was halted as a wave of anticipation rippled through the crowd. Both Eric and Dani had attended enough horse races in their lifetimes to know what that meant – the horses were almost in post positions. A few silent breaths passed and then the flag dropped signaling the start of the race. They were off.

For the first part of the race, they would not be able to see anything. They would have to rely on the pulse

One Race to Ruin 217

of the crowd, the rippling of commentary and energy through the assembled masses. Reactions and emotions traveled even faster than racehorses.

Eric tried not to read too much into the rumblings of the crowd. Beside him, he knew that Taylor had his stopwatch out, tracking the time, thinking in his head where Mercury should be as each second ticked away on his miniature clock. Eric determinedly kept his eyes averted. He would know soon enough.

The horses and jockeys appeared in the distance. They were still too far away to identify or make out positions. All Eric or Dani could tell was that there was a solid group of them in a single huddled mass.

Dani stood on her tiptoes, gripping Eric's hand tightly for support so she did not topple over as she craned her neck to try and see what was happening. She had excellent eyesight, if only she could get a clear view …

"He's at the front!" She shrieked excitedly, squeezing his hand even harder. How such a small woman developed such a strong grip, he would never figure out. But he did not want her to let go.

She was right. As the horses flew down the track, it became clear that what had at first appeared like a tight group of horses and riders was four horses close together but trailing a full length behind the leader. Mercury ran in strides so long and powerful they ate up the ground with seemingly effortless ease. Atop him, Tatum Greene was nothing but a blur of royal blue silks.

Eric and Dani leaned forward against the rail, both of them yelling loudly as Mercury became clear. Not a speck of mud adorned the radiant chestnut's snout or chest. He had run the entire race at the front of the field, never even giving another contender a chance to cover him in mud.

As the horses' hooves ate up the final quarter-mile, a bay colt started to challenge, breaking free of the group and gaining on Mercury's inside shoulder. Eric recognized the horse immediately; it was the horse entered by Bradford Kenner. He felt himself stiffen.

But Dani shook her head. "There's no way!" She exclaimed. "He's got it!"

Mercury seemed to sense that he had a challenger. He flicked his head to the left, caught sight of the other horse, and dug in deeper. He thundered over the finish line, leaving the sorry challenger and his compatriots covered in mud and disappointment.

Dani threw herself into Eric's arms. She wrapped her hands around his neck and kissed him unreservedly, completely oblivious to the whooping and hollering of the crowds around them.

Eric heard her before he saw her. She was speaking in rapid Spanish. He did not understand a word, but he felt certain she was heaping praise upon the colt. He paused halfway down the aisle of the stable.

Dani stood just outside of Mercury's stall, petting and feeding the horse carrots out of her hand. Dappled rays of sunshine were filtering down through the depleted hayloft above, catching strands of her red hair and setting them alight like a flame. Her plum-colored gown, with its perfectly tailored short jacket, shimmered like a jewel. In her hair, gathered in an elegant twist at the nape of her neck, she wore a jeweled pin.

He was completely transfixed. Had it really been just last night that he had kissed her neck, right at the spot where a defiant curl was threatening to break loose? Six hours had passed, maybe seven, since he had watched her dress in this very outfit.

But Eric felt like he was living a different life now.

He must have moved toward her or made some sound – though he didn't do so intentionally – for her head turned and her eyes found him. Her face softened and a look of hopeful eagerness lit her entire countenance with a rosy glow.

Eric had never felt worse in his entire life.

Not when he had discovered the depth of his father's failure to manage their family fortune. Not when he had discovered the deplorable Bradford Kenner was the owner of his debts. Not when he was considering abandoning his values for some future with this magnificent woman. This was it. He had to say goodbye. And he had never dreaded anything more.

"I know I oughtn't to be spoiling him, but he's such a good boy," she said defensively, offering the horse another carrot from her outstretched hand.

Eric tried to smile but the action was painful. He reached up and stroked Mercury's nose. For once, the stubborn horse did not toss his head or resist.

Dani knew immediately that something was amiss. The look on Eric's face did not match the one that had stood outside for the better part of an hour, receiving congratulations and celebrating.

"What's happened?" She asked.

Eric swallowed hard. "We've won the 2000 Guineas."

"Obviously. I thought it was a cause for celebration! It should go a long way towards helping make the estate solvent again ..." she cast her eyes downward, knowing it would make him awkward to speak about but unable to stop herself.

"Yes, you are correct." Eric nodded his agreement, but his expression did not soften. "It is a beginning, but it is only that. Just the beginning."

Mercury nudged her shoulder, looking for another snack. "A marvelous beginning. Now, onto the Derby!" Dani twirled the horse's forelock around her finger affectionately.

"Dani, I appreciate all you have done for Mercury and the stable. For me. However –"

"However?" She cut in, her coppery eyebrows raising sharply.

"It is time that I see you returned to your family." Eric knew the words would hurt her. *Lord knew they hurt him*. But he said them anyway.

Dani opened and closed her mouth in confusion. Some part of her, in the back of her mind ... he had said he did not want to marry her. But now he wanted to throw her over completely?

"You think I should return to my family?"

"Yes."

"To my aunt and uncle?"

"Well –"

"Because I will never return to that house. I will not be treated like a piece of trash. I deserve better than that –"

"Of course you do! I never meant –"

One Race to Ruin

"And yet you treat me no better!" Danie was not close to tears this time. The anger burning and bubbling inside of her was much too hot to allow such a thing. Though she might start blowing steam out of her ears.

"You know I hold you in the highest regard." Even as he said it, Eric knew it sounded feeble and unconvincing.

"But you do not want to marry me. You do not even want to see me anymore. Or allow me to work with Mercury."

"It just isn't possible, Dani. Winning the 2000 Guineas purse helps matters but it will take months, perhaps even years to dig out of the hole that my father left for me. I cannot ask you to wait for that."

"You cannot or you will not?" Beside her, Mercury grunted menacingly, clearly having sided with the beautiful fireball who had won his heart weeks ago.

Eric sighed. "It does not matter."

Dani bit her lip to keep her fiery retort down. "No, I suppose it doesn't," she said instead.

"I will have the horses saddled and brought round, and then I will escort you back to Cambridge." Eric turned away, avoiding her gaze. If he met it, looked too closely at the pain in her eyes, he might cave in and give her what both of them wanted so desperately, but what only he was wise enough to know could not be.

Dani snorted derisively. "I said before: I am not going back to my aunt and uncle's home."

"Then where?"

"I will take the coach to Gainsborough. With the 2000 Guineas over, there will surely be plenty of people taking their leave. I should be able to find overnight accommodations. Then on the morrow, I will book passage back home." She picked up a brush and began running it over Mercury's neck repeatedly, even though she had already thoroughly brushed him out. She just needed something to do so she did not completely lose her wits.

"I cannot let you go to Gainsborough alone."

"For someone determined to no longer be a part of my life, you seem to feel awfully entitled to opinions about it."

"Dani, you are a young, unmarried woman –"

"Who has gained a reputation as a ruinous harlot?" She finished, her voice fairly burning with ire.

Eric knew better than to take that bait. "I insist."

There had to be something she was missing. There just had to be. How could the thoughtful and warm man of the last day have so dramatically transformed? "What aren't you telling me, Eric?"

She was damnably perceptive. Eric knew that if he told her all, Dani would protest and insist they face whatever dangers there were together. But he would not put her in the position to endanger her own life again.

Chapter 26

The rain returned overnight. Daniela waited inside the inn, her bag draped over her shoulder and her arms wrapped tightly around her as she watched the precipitation drenching the street. She had considered slipping out to a different inn, taking a room there, and sneaking onto the coach by herself just to spite Eric.

But in the end practicality won out. She was so wrung out from the day's events that by the time she stumbled into her rented room she'd barely had time to divest herself of her cropped jacket before falling into bed asleep. It seemed impossible and cruel to have experienced such a kaleidoscope of emotions in one twenty-four-hour period. First the joy of lovemaking and the warmth of partnership and closeness, followed by the pride of winning, and then ultimately the betrayal of the one she thought she loved.

In the glow of the aftermath of winning the 2000 Guineas, she had realized that she loved Eric Weathers, Earl of Fordham. He was surly and obstinate most of the time but more than once she had seen his good heart. While most people would have ignored a lowly exercise rider he had accepted Dani's opinions and worth. Although their first meeting as man and woman had been awkward and physically painful – *for him, at least* – he had squired her around Newmarket and rescued her gallantly from her pursuers in the Cambridge town square. But what had really made her fall in love was his commitment to his family's future. He was willing to sacrifice his own happiness and pride to ensure that the future Earls of Fordham would have a name and estate to be proud of one day. It was a gift her father had given to her by building the Rames' family name into one of respect throughout the world of English racing.

She had thought Eric Weathers a man worthy of her love, despite all the nonsense that had been swirling around them.

And just a matter of hours later, he had ripped her heart out and crushed it under his expensive black leather riding boot.

She could not wait to get to Gainsborough. It would take two days by carriage if the horses were fast. She was sure that Eric's would be. Then she would be well shot of him. If he slowed the horses down to a trot so she could jump out, that would be sufficient for her.

Eric arrived promptly at nine o'clock. If his driver recognized the sullen young woman as the same shining sprite from the morning before, he knew better than to comment on it. Daniela did not even wait for Eric to disembark the carriage. If he did, he would try to help her in. He would hold her hand, maybe even touch her waist. And she did not know if she could bear his touch.

She pulled open the door of the carriage and Eric stumbled backward, falling ungracefully onto the seat behind him. She could not help the little smile of satisfaction that tugged at the corners of her mouth. Daniela climbed in, careful to avoid touching him, sat down on the opposite seat, and closed the carriage door behind her with a firm *click*.

He stared at her appraisingly for a moment, trying to determine what to say. At a loss, Eric instead reached up and tapped on the roof of the carriage to signal the driver to go. Daniela crossed her arms, leaned back into the seat, and closed her eyes. She could feign sleep all the way to the midpoint of their trip. At least, she would try.

The well-sprung carriage, purchased before Eric had inherited the title and tightened the estate's purse-strings, glided along the hills and forested roads of the English East Midlands with ease. Eric had made the trip from Newmarket to Doncaster so many times, he could have easily narrated the route. But, of course, Daniela had also grown up on the racing circuit. She knew these roads as well as he. And she wanted nothing to do with him. She had made that abundantly clear from the moment she climbed inside the carriage.

Not that he could blame her. He'd broken her heart. Tossed her over. Ruined her and then spurned her. She had every right to hate him. Hell, he wasn't his own biggest fan right at the moment.

It was the most painfully awkward day of his life. Sitting directly across from the woman who two nights before had been in his bed, whose body he had worshiped, whose spirit he adored. All he wanted to do was pull her into his lap, kiss her, and make passionate love to her as they bounced along these English country roads. He longed to confess every worry in his heart and soul, knowing that she would offer comfort and partnership. And all she wanted to do was ignore him.

They stopped for lunch; his cook in Cambridge had put together a hamper of food. The optimistic woman had even included a bottle of wine and some chocolate – clearly, a feast meant for two. Eric did not even bother taking them out. He handed Daniela a portion of meat, cheese, and bread, offered her some ale, and tried to obey her unstated but nonetheless painfully clear wishes for minimal interaction.

The trip to Gainsborough could not be accomplished in one day. Or rather, it could not be accomplished in one day unless one was willing to ride through the night. Daniela had been all for this. She did not want to spend a moment longer than necessary with Eric. Eric had argued his coachman needed a rest and that had caused Daniela to cave. They stuttered to a stop in front of a tavern inn serving a clientele of travelers.

"I will see about securing lodgings," Eric said as he started to climb out.

"I want my own room." Her voice was as hard as stone.

"I assumed as much."

A mouse was creeping along the floorboards of her room in the tavern. The first few times she heard it, she reacted by rolling over and trying to see what was making the little rustling noise. Naturally, that sent the little creature scurrying back to its refuge somewhere behind the scarred and battered armoire that stood in the corner of the room.

She laid very still. The minutes ticked by. On any other night, Daniela would have been fast asleep by now. She was usually so tired out from riding and caring for the horses that by the time she tumbled into bed, slumber found her quickly. But not tonight.

For a day spent seated in a carriage, it had been utterly exhausting. The energy that it took to avoid touching, interacting, speaking, or even glancing at another person who was seated directly opposite to her was surprisingly substantial. For his part, at least Eric had not tried to push her boundaries. He'd kept his gaze fixed out the window for the majority of the trip so far. When they arrived at the tavern he'd arranged their separate lodgings and had supper sent up to her room.

On any other night, Dani would have been asleep. But she was so desperately lonely that even the idea of the small, furry companion was appealing to her.

She'd never considered herself as someone who needed others to be happy. She and her father were close, surely. How could they not be? Growing up it had just been the two of them and a handful of close family friends. But her father had encouraged and nurtured her independent, self-sufficient nature.

When she went to stay with her aunt and uncle it had been instantly clear that she had astonishingly little in common with the other Rames'. She'd ridden onto Newmarket Heath that day in early spring looking to reestablish her connection with the horses, to reclaim some part of her identity during her forced sojourn in Cambridge.

Then the Earl of Fordham happened. And for the first time in her life, Dani had begun to see what it might feel like to have a partner … someone who truly understood her desires and passions. It was why she had chafed so much at the idea of joining the marriage market with her cousin – because none of those men could possibly understand her. Not like Eric could.

It would be best to go on as she had started this trip. She would keep her distance until they could truly and finally be parted. But the temptation to throw off the coverlet, cross the hall, and fall into Eric's arms again was real and visceral. Somehow, Dani knew that if she did, he would take her into his bed and make her feel that same way again: treasured, respected, adored.

Then the light of morning would come and they would be exactly where they were at this very moment. Broken.

As they crossed into Lincolnshire, Eric's eyes burned from exhaustion. He had not allowed himself to sleep during the ride yesterday. He had insisted on escorting Dani to Gainsborough because he firmly believed a young woman should not travel alone. And though he had seen no sign of the tweed-man or his henchman Eric could not entirely dismiss the possibility that he or Dani would be followed.

He would not be much protection if he was asleep. In his room at the tavern, he'd passed a restless night. While his body laid alone in the lumpy bed, his mind had been fixed on the woman who slept across the hall.

Eric wondered again and again if he was doing the right thing. If he married Dani, he might be able to help her salvage her reputation but he would be subjecting her to a life of strife, living race to race, with the specter of danger always hanging over her. If he did not marry her, she would be able to remain in the security of her father's farm, with friends and family who loved her and could see to her every comfort. Her reputation would likely never recover but she would be safe.

No, he scolded himself. He had made his decision. There was no going back now.

When she opened her eyes again late that afternoon, Daniela was greeted by the familiar stretches of whitewashed fencing that went on for acres along the nearly mile-long drive onto her father's stud farm. The horses here were extremely valuable. The high-strung stallions were kept in separate paddocks with tall fences that the physically fit horses could not easily jump. The mares were kept on the entire other side of the property to avoid temptation. It was a huge operation and a prosperous one.

The long drive had always filled Daniela with warmth and today it did the same despite the troll of a man seated opposite her. She was coming home. She might be bruised and battered from her time away, but home could heal all wounds. Hopefully.

She chanced a glance over at Eric. Did he realize how close they were? He must. While he lived most of his life on the other side of the racing world, he had surely visited a stud farm before. But his face was unreadable. He'd worn that same expression, jaw tight, brow slightly furrowed, and eyes pointed outward, for most of the trip.

The driver slowed the carriage horses from a trot to a walk. Daniela leaned forward and looked out the window as they traveled over the last few dozen yards to the front of the large manor house where she had grown up. Standing between two large stone planters that flanked either side of the house's entrance, arms crossed, was a familiar figure.

The horses lurched to a stop and Daniela nearly jumped from the carriage. She alighted onto the drive with a crunch of gravel beneath her boot. Two steps, three, and she fell into her father's arms, burying her head against his chest.

"I did not know if you would be back yet. I sent a letter …" Dani mumbled against his shoulder.

"I received it." Her father pushed her hair back from her face and pressed a kiss to her forehead.

The gravel crunched again as the Earl of Fordham climbed from the coach. Nathaniel Rames' grip on his daughter tightened.

"Fordham," he growled, keeping Dani firmly locked in his arms.

Eric inclined his head respectfully. "It is a pleasure to meet you at last, Mr. Rames."

"I cannot say the feeling is reciprocated." Nathaniel turned around, taking his daughter firmly by the arm to lead her inside, and left the earl standing quite alone on the doorstep.

Chapter 27

He should not have expected much better.

Eric had no idea what Dani may have told her father or what he may have already heard through other sources. The world of thoroughbred racing in England was painfully small and tight-knit. He debated getting into the carriage and heading right back to Cambridge. But something pulled him inside – *something idiotic, surely* – following the footsteps of father and daughter moments before.

"... your letter this morning. I was preparing to start the journey to Cambridge to retrieve you myself. Then young Jamie rode in and said they'd spotted a carriage out on the Old Mill road."

"We – *I* – left as soon as I could after the 2000 Guineas."

"Dani, you shouldn't have stayed. You should have come straight home ..." Dani's father trailed off as the

One Race to Ruin

Earl of Fordham appeared in the doorway between the foyer and the parlor. The worried look he'd been giving his daughter hardened.

Dani pursed her lips. "You may go now," she said icily.

Eric ignored her. "Mr. Rames, I wished to see Dani – Miss Rames," her father's cheek twitched at the man's casual use of his daughter's name. "I wished to see Miss Rames home safely. Things were not acceptable in Cambridge. She could not remain there any longer."

The tension in Nathaniel's face eased fractionally. "I thank you, Fordham, for removing Daniela from that unconscionable situation. I am appalled at my sister-in-law's behavior and at my brother for allowing such mistreatment." Although they were said begrudgingly, the words were genuine.

"I desire only to protect her, sir."

Nathaniel assessed him again with a deep, penetrating look. When he said nothing more, Eric bowed to both of them.

"I shall be on my way –"

"It is time for you to depart –"

"Perhaps you would rest the night with us here, Fordham –"

"What?"

"It's a kind offer, sir, but –"

"Father, what are you thinking!"

"It's a long journey, Dani, have some pity –"

"I do not wish to cause any discomfort."

"I think you've caused plenty already, Fordham, but it's near dark and we all know the roads are not as safe as they once were." Nathaniel Rames spoke definitively. Dani looked mutinous. She opened her mouth to speak, but the look from her father was enough to stall her.

Dani threw up her hands in exasperation and sauntered from the room with an indignant look on her beautifully pale, sweetly freckled face.

The two men stood silently in her absence. Nathaniel sighed, then walked to the sideboard and poured two snifters of amber-colored spirit. He handed one to Eric as he walked out the door, offering no further comment.

A butler appeared and showed Eric to accommodations upstairs. He told him when the evening meal would be served. *That* was going to be a painfully awkward affair.

Eric knew he was an unwanted guest. But he also was not the type to cower in his room. He changed out of his traveling clothes and went downstairs. He looked into a few rooms but all were deserted except for servants. Dani and her father were the only family members who lived here, he remembered. Nathaniel was surely out on the farm somewhere tending to business. The Lord only knew where Dani was at this moment.

It was a big farm. What were the odds he would encounter her if he went for a walk to stretch his legs after two sedentary days carriage-bound?

Better than they had been on Mercury to win the 2000 Guineas, it turned out.

Despite the distance, Eric recognized the rider galloping along the lane between the paddocks instantly. She had a unique grace. The way she sat a horse – it was as if they had a special language all their own. He had never seen someone who could connect so quickly to their mount.

His heart pounded hard in his chest. She was the most magnificent thing he had ever seen. It was the first time Eric had seen her riding without a specific purpose in mind. He'd seen her skillfully execute Taylor's instructions for riding Mercury through a variety of training runs. They'd ridden together between destinations. But to see her like this … unequivocally free, riding at her own pace, for her own pleasure … it was truly breathtaking.

Eric was not conscious of his feet carrying him towards her, along the parallel line of white fencing. Of course, she was far ahead of him and completely oblivious to his presence. On the morrow, he would leave. Return to Cambridge and continue the work of rebuilding his family's fortunes. But today, he could watch her and enjoy her for just a little while more.

When Eric arrived in the parlor that evening he was surprised to find it deserted. He poked his head in a few doors and eventually wandered into the formal dining room. Dani's father was already seated at the head of the table with a glass of wine in front of him. He did not bother standing when Eric entered the room.

"We are a little less formal here than you are probably used to, Lord Fordham. But the fare is good and the wine is excellent." Nathaniel nodded to an open chair beside him.

Eric took it, accepting a glass of wine from the footman and taking a sip of the deep red liquid. It was, indeed, excellent.

"Daniela will not be joining us tonight."

Eric sighed heavily. "I did not mean to cause her to be uncomfortable in her own home. I will take my meal upstairs." He began to stand up, but Nathaniel shook his head and waved his hand for Eric to stay seated.

"Her old governess is married now to my stable manager and lives with her family on the southeastern corner of the farm. She's gone to visit with them for the evening."

"I see."

"I wanted a chance to speak with you alone."

"I had surmised as much."

Nathaniel chuckled, though without much humor. "Then you're already a cleverer fellow than your father."

Eric tensed. It was not the first time he'd heard the sentiment expressed, but it still burned.

Nathaniel took another long drink of his wine while the first course was served. "Your father was a kind-hearted man and a pleasant chap. But he never seemed to be able to make things work out on the racecourse."

"That is fair," Eric agreed.

"I am trying to piece together, Fordham, what exactly happened in Cambridge," Nathaniel said after a few bites.

One Race to Ruin

Eric laid aside his utensil. "I will answer your questions as best I can, sir."

"In her letter, Dani said she posed as a man, was hired as an exercise rider at your stable at Newmarket, and proceeded to help you train your horse for the 2000 Guineas."

Eric nodded. "That is all true."

"I do not doubt the veracity of my daughter's story, Fordham," he clarified. "What I am not clear on is the details of how things went so wildly amiss. She mentioned some sort of accident, that her identity was revealed, and her aunt was terrible in how she handled the whole matter."

There was nothing Eric could do but nod. Nathaniel narrowed his eyes, watching the younger man closely.

"What is your question, sir?"

"What is my daughter not telling me?"

He had promised to answer Daniela's father's questions. So he must. "I discovered her ruse before the accident. I knew her identity, but I continued to allow her to ride Mercury."

"I see."

"I have done your daughter a great wrong, sir —"

"That is abundantly clear to me."

They sat in silence for several long breaths. "That is not all."

Nathaniel raised his eyebrows, waiting.

"Dani left her aunt and uncle's house the night before the 2000 Guineas. There were no accommodations to be had in Newmarket." Eric met the other man's eyes directly as he said the next part. "She was resident in my house for the night."

Nathaniel's face was a hard mask. Finally, he spoke. "So you will marry her."

Yes! Eric's heart screamed. But he choked it down. "I cannot."

"The only reason I have not called you out is that I received another letter, in the same packet as the one Daniela wrote. From Tatum Greene." Nathaniel's face was reddening though his tone remained level.

"Greene has no allegiance to me."

"No, he does not. And yet, he spoke of you in the most complimentary of terms. He even went so far as to suggest to me that you might make a suitable match for Daniela. But here you sit, telling me you will do no such thing."

"I *cannot* marry her," Eric repeated.

"Why not? It is certainly within my rights to demand it of you … given the rumors swirling out of Newmarket." The older man crossed his arms, the main course on his plate thoroughly ignored.

"You knew my father. Then you can probably imagine the state he left the earldom in. I have spent considerable time and effort to win the 2000 Guineas. It is a victory, to be sure, and a step towards solvency. But it is not enough to guarantee a secure and happy future for me. Or for a wife." Eric leaned forward on the table as he spoke, unintentionally lending emphasis to his words.

Nathaniel's eyebrows maintained their post high on his forehead, but his eyes themselves softened. "She will have a dowry –" he began, but Eric shook his head.

"Pardon me for bringing it up, sir, but Dani confided to me about your troubles here. I do not know the outcome of your trip to Ireland –" Eric saw the older man's face cloud over, "—but I have seen how deeply she loves you and this place. I cannot ask her to give that up, to help me rebuild what may be a hopeless enterprise."

"I do have something to offer." Eric had been thinking about it as they rode along the hills and valleys of English countryside. "Mercury would not have won the 2000 Guineas without Dani helping in his training. The purse is as much hers as mine. More, for what she has sacrificed. When I return to Cambridge I will arrange to have the entirety of the purse transferred to her. I recognize it is not much, not an exchange for her reputation, but it is all I have."

Eric would have to sell off a fair number of horses from his racing string in order to finance the rest of the operation until Mercury could run in the Derby, the next of the Classics for which the colt was qualified. And he would certainly have to let go of some staff from his Cambridge house. But if Dani could live with the shadow of ruin he could certainly get on without a valet or butler.

He had intentionally avoided mentioning the dangerous and unknown origins of Dani's accident to her father. Eric felt certain he would be approached again, whether it be by Kenner or the race-fixing syndicate. The less that he involved Dani and her family, the safer she would be.

Nathaniel stood up, shooing off the footman standing by in the corner, and refilled their wineglasses himself. "It's just like my daughter to get herself into the most impossibly complicated situation fathomable."

Despite himself and the tension of the situation, Eric laughed. Nathaniel himself let out a small chuckle. They sat silently over their food and wine for several minutes, both contemplating their own line of thinking. It was Nathaniel who broke the silence.

"I would like you to stay here on the farm for a few days."

Eric shook his head automatically. "The offer is deeply appreciated, sir, but I do not think that Dani will appreciate my hanging around."

"Consider it a business trip. If you make a successful enterprise of the mess your father left you, you will eventually need to be more familiar with what we do here." When Eric opened his mouth to protest again, Nathaniel added: "I will see to my daughter."

"You have invited him to stay?" Dani asked incredulously, nearly dropping the brush she had been dragging through her hair. She'd only just returned from her afternoon and evening with Emmaline and her family. Her father knocked on her door just as she unpinned her hair and started brushing out the unruly curls.

"He owns an entire stable of racehorses. He has already made the trip all the way here. Might as well do a little business," Nathaniel said matter-of-factly.

"No one asked him to come. I tried to tell him *not* to." Dani realized she was pulling the brush through

One Race to Ruin

her hair with such ferocity, long strands of bright red hair were falling to the floor. *Best to lay that aside for now.*

"Despite that, he is here now."

Dani shook her head, completely at a loss. "I expected you of all people to take my side."

Her father sighed. "I will always take your side, Dani. I wanted to call the man out, force him to marry you. You were the one who insisted that you did not want to marry him."

Dani closed her eyes, trying to keep a hold on the pain that rippled through her. She had indeed told her father that she did not want to marry Eric. Those were the first words out of her mouth once they had been alone in the parlor earlier that afternoon. She had not told her father exactly what had passed between her and Eric but the man was not an idiot. However, it was quite a departure from forcing the man who had ruined to the altar to inviting him to stay at the farm as a guest. *What in the world was her father thinking?*

"I do not want to marry someone who does not want me," Dani finally said quietly.

Nathaniel took his daughter's hand, holding it tightly. As a father, there was nothing in the world quite as debilitating as watching your child in pain. The seedling of an idea formed in his mind as he pulled his daughter close.

Chapter 28

Intent on avoiding Eric as much as possible, Daniela threw herself into the work of the farm. There was always something to do – horses to be exercised and groomed, even stalls to be mucked. It was highly unusual for a woman of good breeding to do such things but Daniela was not deterred. When she had first shown interest in the operation of the farm as a child her father had told her she needed to understand all aspects, even the grosser and more mundane ones. She distinctly remembered the day she had mucked her first stall. Now that she was a grown woman, she could not get by with wearing breeches while she helped out. But an older muslin dress that needed mending anyways served just as well for most barn tasks. She shied away from none of it. It kept her out of Eric's line of sight.

One Race to Ruin

She was not always able to avoid him at meals. Thus far, they had passed one luncheon and two evening suppers together. It had been interminably uncomfortable for everyone involved. Her father was no help at all. In fact, he seemed to like the man! On the third day, Daniela took to praying that today would be the day he left. On the fourth day, Eric practically stumbled over her in the stable. Clearly, the Almighty had a sense of humor.

"Your father suggested I tour the barns today. I believe he was looking for someone to show me around, a Mr. Hanson. But he seems to have gone amiss," Eric offered by way of explanation of his presence.

"Mr. Hanson had to see to an errand in town. You will have to reschedule your tour." She sauntered away from him, intent on ending the conversation there. Her hands tightened into fists when she heard his footsteps following her.

"Perhaps you could show me." Eric was shocked at the words coming out of his mouth. What did he hope to achieve by forcing his companionship on her? Was it not torture enough to them both? But he could not resist. He missed her.

Dani stopped abruptly in the middle of the aisle. So abruptly, Eric nearly crashed into her. He kept his feet but reached out instinctively to steady himself, his hand landing on her shoulder. It was a warm day and she wore a thin, light tan muslin gown. He could feel the heat of her body through the nearly sheer fabric. He was close enough to see the freckles sprinkled across the bridge of her nose.

Her heart was hammering her chest. Dani shivered, but not quite the enjoyable, tantalizing kind.

This was a painful mixture of longing, anticipation, and debilitating sadness.

"I cannot," she said quietly, hating how vulnerable she sounded.

Eric quickly removed his hand, clasping them behind his back awkwardly. He took a step back and looked quickly from side to side, casting about for something to say or do to break the tension. His eyes fell on the stallion whose stall they had stopped in front of: a wide chested dark bay thoroughbred with a distinct lightning-shaped white blaze on his forehead.

Stepping closer to see in the dim lighting of the barn, Eric could scarcely believe his eyes. "Is that Windstorm?"

A self-satisfied look crept onto Dani's face. "It is," she confirmed, leaning down to pick up a bucket of water that had been left in the aisle and pouring it carefully into the magnificent stallion's trough.

"I heard he had been sold to a private stable, that he was not available for breeding –"

"He's not available." She continued refilling to the water trough, keeping her eyes determinedly turned away.

"What do you mean?"

"He's mine. He was a gift for my eighteenth birthday. He's not a part of the farm's stock. I have complete control of his breeding rights."

"I see. Has he sired any foals yet?"

"Just one. With my mare, Verity. Born last season." Done with her chores, Dani stepped back from the stall and dusted off her hands on her skirt.

"I'd love to see the foal."

One Race to Ruin 245

Dani gritted her teeth. Her father had insisted this was now a business trip for Eric. That did not mean *she* had to do any business with him. However, she was very proud of the little colt that Verity and Windstorm had produced. She couldn't resist showing him off.

"Come on, then." She walked quickly down the aisle and across the stable yard. Eric could have easily kept up but he tried to give her space. Dani led him along the outside of two fenced paddocks, then into another stable yard and smaller barn.

The inside was dim and a sense of calm permeated the space. This was where they kept the broodmares and their young, Eric realized as they walked down the rows of stalls. Verity was in the very last stall on the right. Dani stopped, leaning forward onto the stall door.

"Buenos dias mis corazoncitos. ¿Cómo están hoy?" She crooned. Verity came forward and nuzzled Dani's shoulder. Dani held out her hand and the foal stepped into the light.

He was a perfect miniature of his father. His dark coat shined like onyx where it caught the sunlight. Already, Eric could see his impeccable conformation.

"He's perfect."

Dani smiled appreciatively. "Thank you."

"Is he already sold?"

She shook her head, the same sunlight that made the foal's coat shine making her long locks gleam as well. Eric felt that familiar lurch of sadness in his stomach. He could not have her, he reminded himself.

"I am going to keep him and train him myself. Doncaster is not far from here. I will let a stall and find a trainer. My father does not have much interest in racing himself but I would like to try my hand at it."

"You will be a success, I am sure of it," Eric said loyally. He leaned closer to get a better view of the foal. The young colt was perfect. Dani came to stand beside him, a proud smile on her face. Her expression was softer and more relaxed than Eric had seen her in days.

Their arms touched, the length from their wrists to elbows where they both leaned on the stall door. Eric could not tear his eyes away from her. Then she turned to look up at him and their faces were separated by mere inches.

Neither of them knew who initiated it, nor did it matter. They were like magnets being pulled together. A force which could not be denied. Eric pushed rational thought aside and tried to enjoy the taste of her, painfully aware it would be his last. He drew his tongue slowly along her lips, first the bottom, fuller and pouted outwards. Then the top, with its perfectly bow-shaped curve. She was leaning into him, her body seeking his.

Eric's hands found her waist, the soft curve of her hip separated from his fingertips only by a few layers of thin fabric. Dani gripped his arms, holding them tightly as she stumbled backward. Her lips never leaving his, she led him across the aisle to where several empty stalls stood in shadows. She reached up and fumbled with the latch on one of the empty stalls. Eric's lips had left hers and were kissing her neck and throat, his tongue drawing hot circles on her tender skin, his teeth nipping and sending waves of heat through her. She whimpered, thrusting her hips forward, desperately seeking closeness.

One Race to Ruin

They staggered together into the darkness of the stall, their hands too busy touching every inch of the other's body to bother trying to hold on or find a steadying handhold. Eric was at the neckline of her gown, his tongue assaulting her breasts. Dani's hands moved from his shoulders down to his hips. She pulled impatiently at the fasteners of his breeches, tugging the material out of the way so she could expose him. Her hand encircled him, rubbing from base to tip and back again.

They were both completely swept away. Eric pulled up her skirt, Dani helped him ruck it up around her waist. He plunged two fingers inside of her. She cried out, then bit her lip hard to hold in the sound. Finding her wet and ready, he could not wait another minute. He withdrew his hand and replaced it with his hot cock.

With every thrust, Dani was pushed up against the tall wooden wall of the stall. The unforgiving wood was a stark contrast to the softness of a bed; it allowed him to get deeper, to take her harder. She was coming to the edge more quickly too. Her hands slid beneath his jacket, gripping his shoulders. Her fingernails dug into his skin through the thin linen of his shirt.

"Ah, ahhhhhhhh!" The cries tore from her, escaping her attempts to hold them in check. Somehow aware – amidst the throes of passion – that someone might hear them, Eric covered her mouth with his and kissed her deeply. He kept his mouth fastened to hers as she tightened, shuddered, and then relaxed against him. He felt his climax coming seconds later, his hips thrusting hard and fast as he filled her completely.

Their mouths finally broke apart. They were both gasping for breath. Dani slid her hands from beneath his jacket. They were trembling. Eric wanted to reach out and take them into his own to steady them – but she wrapped her arms around herself before he could. He stepped back, releasing her hips. Her skirts fell back into place. Eric adjusted his breeches and his shirt.

Dani was chewing her bottom lip aggressively, an inscrutable look upon her face. She peeked into the aisle, relaxing fractionally when she found it still deserted. She turned her eyes up to meet his. In the shadowy light, his blue eyes were tinted to a soft gray. She could have happily spent the rest of her life gazing into those eyes. But some things were not meant to be.

She shook her head sadly. "I suppose that was goodbye."

Chapter 29

It was time to go. What had happened in the barn was proof that he could not trust himself around her. He wanted her too much. It was time to rip away the bandage and let both of them get on with their lives.

Waiting until he was sure Dani had enough time to disappear in whichever direction suited her, Eric walked directly from the barn back up to the main house. He would pack his things, find Nathaniel Rames to thank him for his generosity of spirit, and then he would be gone. Before the evening meal.

He walked inside and started for the stairs to the next floor. He was so singularly focused he did not even notice the butler standing in the hall.

"Fordham?"

Eric paused, his foot already on the first step. The voice had come from the back of the house. Turning slowly, he walked towards it.

He found Dani's father in a small room nestled between the parlor and the library, a compact office filled with a mélange of bookshelves holding leather-bound ledgers. The older man sat behind a work desk opposite an assortment of mismatched chairs.

Nathaniel wore a petite pair of spectacles and was carefully examining a paper in front of him, but he set it aside when Eric came in. "Do you have a moment?"

"Of course, sir. I was just headed upstairs to begin packing."

"Packing?"

"Yes. It is time for me to return to Cambridge," Eric said.

"I see." Nathaniel pulled the spectacles down his nose, his eyebrows raised. "Perhaps you could spare me a few minutes of your time before you are on your way."

Feeling a bit like a child being chastened, Eric sat down in one of the chairs opposite the desk. "I have learned so much in just the past few days, Mr. Rames. I am most thankful for the opportunity."

Nathaniel nodded slowly. "I have also been watching carefully these last few days, Fordham. And it is clear to me that both you and my daughter hold deep feelings for each other."

Eric was stunned by the man's frank appraisal of the situation.

"It is also my opinion that you have made the wrong choice, though for the right reasons."

Nathaniel pushed his glasses back into place and leaned forward over his desk while Eric stared in surprised silence. He shifted a stack of papers to the side, retrieving one particular packet, which he handed across the desk to Eric.

Confused, Eric accepted the pages and leafed through them. His eyebrows raised even higher than Nathaniel's had moments before.

"Where did you obtain these documents?" He asked, more than a little concerned about how Dani's father had obtained detailed documentation of the financial accounts associated with the Earl of Fordham's racing stable.

"I sent word to my solicitor in London, who reached out to your representatives with a proposal. These arrived this morning. I've spent the better part of the day reviewing them." Nathaniel removed his spectacles now, setting them on the desk and leaning back in his leather chair.

"What kind of proposal?" Though there were limited possibilities.

"Before I get to that, I owe you an accounting of what happened in Ireland. The lord there would not relent in his claims. I settled matters by buying back the horse he claimed I had sold to him fraudulently."

Eric nodded along. "That seems a reasonable resolution of the situation."

Nathaniel sighed. "The price was far from reasonable. Many times what the animal was sold for originally. However, it was a necessary outlay to protect the farm. These," he reached for another sheaf of papers and handed them to Eric, "are an accounting of the financial status of the farm and all of the associated assets."

Eric accepted them, looking over the papers page by page. After several minutes, he looked back up at

Nathaniel. He thought he knew what was coming but he needed to hear it. "Why are you showing me these?"

"Because if we are to be partners, we must enter into this venture with clear eyes and a coherent vision for the future."

"A combined enterprise," Eric said slowly, his brain starting to work out the particulars.

Nathaniel elaborated. "We breed horses here, you train and race them through your stable, and then once they've run a profitable career, we put them to stud back on the farm. Of course, there will always be some amount of buying and selling to outside parties. But the animals with the most potential would remain within our control."

"It's a fascinating idea. I cannot see how it would be anything but profitable."

"I agree."

"But, sir … why? There are countless other owners you could approach with this proposal."

Dani's father cocked a half-smile. "There are, I am sure. But none of them are in love with my daughter."

Eric opened his mouth to protest. He closed it and then opened it again, like a fish gulping for water. It was less than dignified, and the older man across the desk couldn't help but chuckle.

"I don't mean to make you feel uncomfortable, Fordham. But if you are amenable, I can send word immediately to have the paperwork drawn up."

The temptation was so painfully real it felt like grating over an open wound. Eric shook his head. He saw the look of surprise on Nathaniel's face and realized that he could keep his secrets no longer.

One Race to Ruin

"It is an intriguing offer, Mr. Rames. And certain to be a profitable one to the right man. But it is one I cannot accept."

Nathaniel looked truly shocked, but Eric continued before the older man could speak. "Dani's accident … it was not an accident, sir. Someone cut the strap on her saddle."

Her father's face paled. "Why would someone do that?"

"It would appear that I have enemies. The man who holds most of my debt – a horrible creature named Kenner. But not long before the 2000 Guineas I was approached by a man who offered incentive for me to fix the outcome."

"Race fixing? Tampering?" Nathaniel leaned back in his chair as a sigh rippled through his solid frame.

"I did not do it, obviously."

"No, your horse ran the race of a lifetime." The older man was stroking his jaw, contemplating. "The debts could be paid off and this fellow Kenner done away with as part of business merger. But race fixing … *hell*, there are reasons I have never gotten involved in the front end of racing."

Realization dawned on Nathaniel's face. He cocked his head to the side and looked at Eric with new appreciation. "That is why you refused to marry Dani."

Eric met the man's eyes and nodded. "I will do anything to keep her safe. Even if it means walking away."

"That's an admirable sentiment but also a damnably stupid one."

"I beg your pardon?"

"She's already in danger. She fell off a horse, for Christ's sake."

"And becoming my wife will only make it worse."

"Or it will lend her the protection of not just one great English racing family, but two." Nathaniel uncrossed his arms and laid them palm down on the table. "You said you were leaving. Your options have changed. What are you going to do now?"

Eric felt something new take hold inside of him … something he had struggled to find for a long time: hope.

He found her standing at the edge of the paddock nearest to the house. Inside the fence were two horses grazing peacefully. It was an image from a dream: the verdant English countryside, the horses' glistening coats, her hair and skin shining luminously.

His footsteps were muffled on the grass but Dani seemed to sense that he was near. She turned around, leaning back on the fence, her hands clasped together tightly in front of her. As he approached she started shaking her head. "Eric, you have to go. I cannot keep doing this … it is tearing me apart …"

"I know," he said. "I am sorry for that. For all of the pain I have caused you." He thought he saw tears welling up in her eyes. He had never seen her cry before. "Let me make it right," he said softly.

As Eric knelt before her, he had the overwhelming sense that things were finally coming to rights

One Race to Ruin

between them. He did not have a marriage ring to offer her so he settled for taking her hand in his own.

"Daniela, will you marry me?" He gazed up at her, glistening red locks falling around her face in the fading rays of early evening sunshine. He watched as a maelstrom of emotions played across her face.

"No."

Eric nearly fell over. "No?"

Dani pulled her hand free and started backing away. She was shaking her head. "No." She repeated.

"I do not understand …"

"That much is very clear." Dani pressed her fingertips to her temples, massaging the delicate skin as if her brain could not process what was happening to her.

Eric cleared his throat awkwardly. He was still kneeling on the ground. Despite his size, he came to his feet gracefully.

"Your father has offered me a partnership. Now I admit, it will not be easy, but —"

"Less than a week ago, you refused to marry me because of my father. Now you are saying you want to marry me because of something my father has offered you?"

Put in terms like that, Eric could understand her chagrin. He opened his mouth to explain but Dani was shaking her head even more emphatically, her chestnut curls bouncing angrily.

"What has changed since the 2000 Guineas?" She demanded. When he didn't immediately respond, she raised her eyebrows and crossed her arms. "Just the financial situation?"

Eric felt his stomach clench. He had spent the better part of an hour talking with her father and then musing on his own. They had hammered out the particulars of a plan not just to merge their racing enterprises, but to protect the one thing that mattered the most to both of them: Dani. With the combined influence and power of their two estates and the profit they would reap, he would be able to protect her. But Nathaniel and Eric had also agreed that it was best not to tell Dani about the race fixing scheme.

He struggled to find the words to reassure her. "This changes everything, Dani. I told you I would not gamble with your well-being and now we won't have to."

"It's not enough."

She stood there a few moments longer, staring directly at him as if daring him to bring forward some other argument that she could systematically dismantle. When he said nothing, she tossed her long red mane over her shoulder and strode away, not bothering to give him a second glance.

Chapter 30

Dani walked from one side of the farm to the other. Even though it was getting dark, she had no jacket or cloak, and the evening air held a distinct chill. She did not know who she was more frustrated with: her father or Eric.

Her father had always been her staunchest ally. For seventeen years of her life, it had been just the two of them. Dani had few memories of her mother, only portraits and a handful of written mementos. She had *known* her father would take her side, protect her, despite what society or the other members of the family might say. And he had, she supposed. He'd not said a word of reproach to her, although he knew most of the story. But he had also kept Eric around, clearly with this ridiculous notion of joining their businesses together. He must think he was doing the right thing – laying plans, securing her future. *Why couldn't a man just talk to the woman in his life and ask her what she wanted?*

Eric was worse. First, he refused to consider marriage, then he made passionate love to her, then he insisted on escorting her home, and now he was suddenly ready to propose? It was preposterous. *The man had no idea what was going on in his own mind!* And the last thing that Dani wanted was to be a burden. She would marry a man who wanted her, who cared for her deeply the way she cared for him, or she would not marry at all.

She needed to get away. Her father's farm, while a place of safety and security, apparently was just not far enough from the scandal and its tentacles, which seemed determined to follow her. A thought occurred to her … *there was one other place she could go.* Sure, she had never been there before. But she had always planned on it. Why not now?

Eric looked around the room, taking in the open trunks, the maid that had just hurried out the door, the clothes thrown about here and there. A cold lump formed in his throat. "Why are you packing?"

Dani did not pause. She continued sorting through the boots that the maid had pulled out of the armoire. She would take the riding ones, of course. But she must also take a sturdy walking pair. She did not know much about the terrain of Spain but it was best to be prepared.

"I am going to stay with my grandparents in Pamplona."

"In Spain."

"*Sí.*"

The word cut him like a knife. But it shouldn't have, he realized. She'd turned down his proposal. And all of the reasons she had given for doing so were perfectly valid. That was what he had come here to say: that he understood why she had said no, and to tell her everything. The full truth. *Because dammit, he wanted her as his wife.* So badly it physically hurt to consider any other possibility.

"Don't leave."

Dani threw down the petticoat she was holding in her hand. It landed on the coverlet of the bed with a satisfying *snap*. She rounded on him, her flaming hair around her face and her hands on her hips. "Tell me why."

"What?" Eric took a defensive step backward.

"Tell me why I shouldn't leave," she said matter-of-factly.

Eric stared at her. *Because he wanted her to be his wife. Because he wanted a future with her. Because ...*

She cut brutally into his thoughts.

"Fine. I am going." She turned back to her task, tossing another pair of boots into her trunk and then continuing down the bed to examine the selection of evening gowns her maid had laid out.

"What do you think you will find in Spain?" Eric moved closer, regaining the step he had lost.

"Well, for one, the whole of Spanish society will not consider me a ruined woman."

"I offered to marry you," Eric tossed back.

"Only after my father made it financially pragmatic for you to do so!" Her dark eyes were gleaming, somehow reflecting the fiery halo of her curls.

"I've wanted to marry you for weeks!" He yelled.

The maid stumbled in the doorway, dropping the pile of hat boxes she had been carrying. She took one look at the expressions on the two young people's faces and prudently decided to retreat.

"Excuse me?" Daniela managed to choke out.

"I wanted to ask you to be my wife the morning of the 2000 Guineas. The night before." He was so exasperated, he threw his hands up into the air.

"Then why didn't you?" She demanded.

"Because there was no future for you as my wife! I am an earl without a fortune, a thoroughbred owner living from race to race. What kind of life is that for you?"

Daniela rolled her eyes so emphatically Eric thought they might get stuck. "You always seem to think you know what is best."

"I was trying to protect you."

"By keeping both of us from the thing we truly wanted?" She asked incredulously. "*Realmente eres un idiota. Un terco, burro de un hombre que no puede* –"

"Yes. All of that," Eric agreed.

Dani's eyebrows shot up.

"I should have told you what happened with Mercury as soon as I found out. I should have run after you that day at Newmarket when your identity was revealed. I did this all wrong from the start."

Daniela froze, her hand gripped around a fistful of muslin. "What are you talking about?"

One Race to Ruin

"Two men approached me the week before the 2000 Guineas. They offered me a substantial sum to throw the race. To cheat."

"And you said no!"

"Of course I did. Then someone cut the girth on your saddle."

Dani dropped the dress she was holding as the pieces of the story clicked together in her mind. "Why didn't you tell me?"

"I was not sure who had done it. Bradford Kenner bought up most of my debts. He certainly had incentive. But so did the men I refused. I did not plan on keeping it from you but things happened so quickly and then I did not want to put you in any more danger." Eric reached out for her hand and was more than a little surprised when Dani did not protest. He ran his thumb over her knuckles. "Will you forgive me?"

She frowned and swatted at his hand. "You and my father cannot go on like this. You must tell me things. I am not a wilting flower. I can handle myself. Haven't I proven that?"

"Yes, more than."

She still did not smile, but she also did not pull her hand away.

"I want to marry you," Eric said plainly.

Her face remained inscrutable. "Tell me why."

"Dammit, you know why." He moved closer, tentatively, to see if she would retreat. But she stayed put, her eyes now locked on his.

"I need to hear you say it," Dani said softly. Her lips were parted, her breath coming in ragged movements. Her chest moved up and down again and again.

He was close enough to touch her now. One hand raised to her face, he stroked his fingertips from her eyebrow down to her chin. Catching his thumb underneath her chin, he tilted her face up to his, leaning down so that his mouth was only a few inches from hers. "You just want to win."

"For once, this has nothing to do with winning."

His mouth came down on hers in a crushing kiss. Dani opened her mouth to him, reaching for Eric with all of the energy and discontent of the last few days. She slid her hand around his neck, pulling herself up so that her toes were almost dangling off the ground. With his solid build and strong arms around her, he hardly noticed her weight. She pulled back and stared up at him, her eyes full of expectation and longing.

"I love you."

Her eyes fluttered closed, letting his words warm her. For once, she did not blush. "I love you, Eric. So much it hurts."

What could he do then but kiss her? He pulled her into his arms and planted another ardent kiss on her waiting lips. The bed behind them was covered with clothes from her interrupted packing, but Eric was ready to throw all of those to the floor and show her just how much he loved and adored her.

Dani pulled back, laughing, a wide smile on her luscious lips, pink and plump from his kiss. "My father is downstairs," she said, nodding towards the door the maid had very thoughtfully closed behind her.

Eric ran his tongue along the sensitive swath of skin beneath her ear to the hollow of her throat. "It's a good thing you are already ruined."

Chapter 31

He was shown first into a shadowed library. It was not the place he usually reported to his employer. Customarily, they met in the backroom of an upscale bordello not far from Hyde Park. Tonight, he had been summoned to the lord's private residence. That must be a good sign.

His attempts to bring the Earl of Fordham on board had come to nothing. He knew his employer was disappointed. The amount of money wagered on a race like the 2000 Guineas, the first of the Classics, was staggering. It followed that the potential for profit if one could put their hand on the scales …

But there were still four races left. An entire racing season. Plenty of time to make up for the loss. He hoped. Maybe this was not as promising of a visit as he had thought –

"His lordship will see you now."

The small man nearly jumped out of his polished leather shoes. He hastily tried to cover his surprise. The butler who had shown him in originally was imperturbable. The black-clad man simply held out his hand to motion through an open door.

Had that door been open the entire time? How had he failed to notice that? Acute observation was a prerequisite of his current position.

"Enter."

Jumping for a second time, he hurried into the room. The door closed behind him, as if by its own volition. This room, like the first, was dimly lit. There was a huge wooden desk, a full six feet long and two feet wide. But no one sat behind it.

He turned slowly, realizing that the room's other occupant was seated behind him in a tall wingback chair in the corner of the room. Proud of his manners even under pressure, the nervous man bowed formally.

"My lord, I have much to tell you –"

"Why did you not secure the Earl of Fordham's cooperation?"

His stomach clenched but he managed to get out a response. "We applied pressure quite insistently, my lord. The young woman –"

"Was a tool you did not utilize effectively," the deep voice cut in. *"Their engagement announcement was in this morning's newspaper."*

"We did arrange for her identity to be revealed, and the ensuing scandal should have been enough to sway the Earl." The man was arguing for his life and he knew it. This line of work was extremely lucrative, but one misstep and the consequences were dire.

"Should have."

One Race to Ruin

Although his insides were quivering, he forced himself to take a deep breath. He must try a different tack. "My lord, there are still four Classics left. I will ensure –"

"You will ensure nothing. This matter will be handed off into more capable hands."

He wanted to argue. It had taken him years to earn his employer's trust, to work his way up within the organization and –

"You shall be thankful that your punishment is not of a more permanent nature."

The argument he had been building in his chest deflated instantly. He swallowed hard. "Thank you, my lord," he managed quietly.

"You are dismissed."

Wanting to say more and yet far too terrified to do so, he bowed again and then backed out of the room, careful never to take his eyes off of the seated man. When the door to the inner room closed, a wave of relief flowed through him. He finally turned around, almost running from the room. He turned the corner too sharply and the sleeve of his jacket caught on the edge of a bronze statue, tearing open the tweed fabric.

But he did not pause to examine the damage. He had to get out of here, out of London, maybe even out of England, as quickly as he could.

Epilogue

All eyes were on them at the Derby Festival. Just as before, Daniela paid little heed to the curious glances of onlookers as she made her way through the crowded racecourse on Eric's arm. She was sure her Aunt Millie and Uncle Baxter were somewhere in the fray. Winnie had mentioned the trip in her last letter. Bringing her hand up to rest atop where her other was tucked into Eric's arm, Daniela stroked her finger absently over the gold engagement ring on her fourth finger. While to the rest of society the ring had restored Daniela to respectability, she doubted that her aunt would look upon it quite so favorably.

"Taylor is waiting for us just over there." Eric nodded across the crowded green. Daniela lifted her hand in greeting as they navigated through the throng of people. They did not have a horse entered in the

One Race to Ruin

Oaks but it was always an exciting race just the same. And tomorrow Mercury would run in the Derby.

"Miss Rames, I am pleased that you were able to join us." Taylor bowed very respectfully. Daniela giggled.

"Mr. Taylor, I have told you again and again that you must call me Dani. Anything else just seems quite wrong from your lips," she admonished.

Taylor smiled sheepishly.

"Besides, Miss Rames won't be accurate for much longer," Eric added, pulling her a little closer against him. "In less than two weeks she will be the Countess of Fordham."

"Yes, about that. Greene and I have talked, and while we appreciate the invitation we feel it would be most inappropriate –"

"Do not dare finish that sentence! I will not hear it!" Daniela put up her hand to reinforce her words. "What is Tatum thinking? I will find him myself and box his ears for spouting such nonsense ..." Spotting the jockey a few yards away chatting, Daniela disentangled her arm and started in his direction.

"I see that donning dresses has not changed her temperament a bit."

Eric shook his head, a silent chuckle shaking his chest. "No, I would say it has emboldened her." He watched his fiancée as she scolded the older man, thankful that for once he was not the target of her ire. He turned to survey the horses being warmed up for the next race. "Anyone of interest running today?"

Taylor took a long draw from his pipe and released a circle of smoke. "The Duke of Redding's boy has entered an interesting filly. Rumor has it that he won the horse over a game of whist."

"That sounds like Will."

"You know the boy?"

"I would not call him a boy. He must be nearing five and twenty. But yes, we are acquainted. He was a few years behind me at school. He always had an eye for the fillies." Eric said sarcastically. He scanned the crowd, his eyes lighting on the subject of their discussion – the dark-haired, dark-eyed young duke-to-be who had been making waves since the moment he left the nursery.

Eric recalled the one time they had both set their sights on the same young widow … it was not a memory that deserved exploring. Especially as Eric felt the touch of his future wife's hand on his arm.

"What are you discussing?" Dani asked innocently. Taylor cleared his throat, mumbling something incoherent under his breath as he turned away.

"The future Duke of Redding." Eric inclined his head towards the young lord who stood with a pack of his friends around a very well-apportioned gray filly.

Dani's eyes narrowed. "They are saying the most unflattering things about him in the ladies' retiring room."

"That does not surprise me in the least."

She tilted her head to one side, considering. A wayward red curl had broken loose from the chignon at the back of her neck and dangled tantalizingly around the hollow of her throat. Eric swallowed hard.

"Perhaps we should not be so quick to judge. We are not exactly the picture of propriety ourselves." Dani squeezed his arm and shot him a look as she spoke, making it quite clear that she knew exactly the direction of her fiancé's mind.

One Race to Ruin

"Perhaps you would like to dress in breeches and see if you can get to the bottom of the scandal." He leaned down and placed a chaste kiss on the tip of her freckled nose.

"I was thinking of saving those for the wedding night, since they seem to be a particular favorite of yours," she purred, sliding her fingers discreetly inside the opening of his tailcoat.

"You minx." Eric glanced around but by some miracle no one seemed to be looking in their direction.

"I prefer hoyden." Dani said sweetly as she raked her thumb over his nipple through the thin linen of his shirt.

Eric cleared his throat to cover the yelp that escaped as Dani touched him. "Hoyden on a hellion. If you ever write your memoirs, that should be your title." He slid his hand up her arm where it was linked with his, rubbing his knuckles firmly against the underside of her breast.

"I thought you were warming towards Mercury?" She bit her lip in a little half smile in part to keep from laughing aloud and in part to keep in a little moan.

"Ask me after tomorrow's race," Eric said between gritted teeth. Dani had moved closer to him, the fullness of her skirt hiding the way she was gently rubbing her hip against him. He felt himself hardening.

"Would you like to show me the stable block you've leased here at Epsom? They ought to be quite deserted just now with the race about to start." Dani licked her lips between sentences.

"We will miss the race," Eric said with only a hint of disappointment.

Dani threw back her head and laughed, her graceful neck and enticing white breasts providing all the convincing that Eric needed. Slipping her arm free, she caught his hand in hers as she started walking away from the track. "There will always be another race, *mi amor*."

"I will happily miss them all to ruin you, my sweet."

The End

If you enjoyed *One Race to Ruin*…

Please leave a positive review on Amazon or Goodreads

Reviews are essential for independent authors! As an emerging author, I read every review you write and take it to heart as I dream up new romances. Your review really does make an impact. It helps other readers find and enjoy these characters and their stories. Thank you for your time. -Cara

Also by Cara Maxwell

The Hesitant Husbands

Meant to be Mine

Love Once Lost

A Love Match for the Marquess

A Very Viscount Christmas (coming Nov. 2021)

Visit caramaxwellromance.com for free content, previews of upcoming books and special offers. Follow @caramaxwellromance on Instagram for updates and exclusive content.

Acknowledgements

Some of my first memories are at the racetrack. While most of the races here are run on dirt rather than turf and the differences between American and British horseracing are never ending (which I only discovered when I began researching this book!) my love of horses and racing made this book so much fun to write. And I have one person to thank for that: my dad. He taught me to read the racing form, to place a bet, and answered every question along the way. Aside from being one of my best friends, he is an incredibly generous and loving person who has always believed in this crazy dream of mine. So thanks, Dad. This one's for you.

To Ashley and Nicole, who did not give me a hard time for working on this book while I was supposed to be on vacation. I love you forever.

To Fenna Edgewood, historical romance author and my dear friend. Thank you for being my first reader, for encouraging me to stay true to my voice, and for being a sounding board for all of my trials and victories. Your friendship is one of the coolest and most unexpected gifts to come from this journey.

About the Author

Bringing fresh perspective and punch to the genre readers already know and love, Cara Maxwell is dedicated to writing spirited heroines and irresistible rogues who you will root for every time. A lifetime reader of romance, Cara put pen to paper (or rather, fingers to keyboard) in 2019 and published her first book. She hasn't slowed down from there.

Cara is an avid traveler. As she explores new places, she imagines her characters walking hand-in-hand down a cobblestone path or sharing a passionate kiss in a secluded alcove. Cara is living out her own happily ever after in Seattle, Washington, where she resides with her husband, daughter, and two cats, RoseArt and Etch-a-Sketch.

Printed in Great Britain
by Amazon